She traveled millions of miles to Mars, only to be left behind on the ship...

Confined to a spaceship orbiting Mars in 2050, astrogeologist Morgan Zeller watches the main lander descend toward the red planet without her. Her disappointment would be less painful if the crew didn't resent how she had ruined their mission. Because she turned up pregnant, NASA canceled their experiments so that Morgan can return to Earth before her child is born. But when the lander crashes, endangering the baby's father, Medical Officer Randall Arnold, and her other crewmates, which include Randy's ex-lover, Morgan takes off in the emergency lander to rescue them.

During the descent, she sees a mysterious flash of light in the Columbia Hills and later discovers alien artifacts there. Her discovery triggers a colonization race among countries that are fighting over territory on the moon. How can Morgan stop them from bringing war to Mars while she copes with pregnancy and a jealous rival?

Mission Control wanted her to do…*what*?

Morgan stepped around to the viewport and asked, "Are you guys okay?"

Diego held up a sign: *Air leaking. Two hours left. Can't reach suits. Vlad unconscious.*

Her heart skipped. "Was the tank punctured?"

He nodded and held up another sign: *Air lock controls damaged. Need door unlatched to get suits.*

"Morgan, what's going on?" Cass asked. "What tank? You're supposed to be taking a break, but your heart rate and blood pressure just increased."

"Cardinal has an oxygen leak, with only two hours of air left. Vlad is unconscious. The crew can't reach their suits in the air lock until I unlatch the inner door manually."

"You need to come back and let me go down there. Your vitals keep changing. If your nausea gets worse, you could regurgitate something into your air supply and—"

"I know the risks. The digging will take longer than I calculated, at least an extra half hour."

Aiden and Jamese reappeared in the window. He looked scared. She glared at Morgan as if blaming her for their plight.

"Morgan, I have to give you this message from Mission Control," Cass said in an odd, stilted voice. "They're glad you have some good news, but they want you to leave the emergency supplies, return to the ship, and let me go down."

In the window, Aiden looked shocked, as if someone had punched him in the stomach. Jamese's face twisted in rage. They could do the math in their heads. The oxygen wouldn't last for everyone. Mission Control had asked if they could get to their suits but didn't wait for an answer before sending the message. The government would rather make martyrs of the trapped astronauts than risk the bad publicity if Morgan's baby didn't survive.

Morgan had no choice. Her shipmates needed help. She couldn't let any of them die to save her baby or herself. "They won't all live until you get here," she told Cass.

KUDOS for *Spaceborn*

In *Spaceborn* by Bonnie Vaughan Morgan Zeller's entire life changes the blink of an eye and in ways she never imagined. Her best friend Sandi is lying in a hospital bed and there is only 3 hours before launch of the spaceship to Mars. The flight would not/could not be delayed. So Morgan did the only thing she could do, she took her friend's place on the mission. But would the crew give her a chance? Would they accept her as part of the team?...But there are a few more little secrets no one was expecting that could jeopardize everything they had all worked so hard for and could tear Randy and Morgan apart forever. And only one person who can save them—Morgan. *Spaceborn* is a page-turner and I enjoyed it very much. – *Taylor Jones, Reviewer*

Spaceborn by Bonnie Vaughan is a fast-paced, hard-hitting, science fiction suspense/thriller. The story revolves around Morgan Zeller, an astrogeologist, who is pregnant and doesn't know it. The space-program doctor, for reasons of his own, doesn't tell her and allows her to board a spaceship on its way to Mars. The baby's father is also among the spaceship crew, though when Morgan finds out she's pregnant, she doesn't tell him. She doesn't know how he will take the knowledge that their one-night stand had unforeseen consequences and she also does not want to ruin her career...I found Spaceborn not only interesting but educational. For instance, it had never occurred to me that when someone bleeds in zero gravity, you have to vacuum up the blood. So I'm impressed. Vaughan obviously did her homework. The plot is exciting and intriguing and the book is hard to put down. – *Regan Murphy, Reviewer*

A great story with rich characters. This is a book you pick up and you don't put down. – *Best-Selling Author, Bonnie Hearn Hill*

ACKNOWLEDGEMENTS

Many thanks to my writing instructors, especially Bonnie Hearn Hill, and to all the people in my writing classes and critique groups who provided feedback on this book.

Thanks to my daughter-in-law Katherine Vaughan for the stunning cover and to my son Chris Vaughan for editing early drafts.

Thanks also to my family, friends, and members of the California Writers Club and the National Association of American Pen Women for their encouragement and support.

SPACEBORN

Bonnie Vaughan

A BLACK OPAL BOOKS PUBLICATION

GENRE: SCIENCE FICTION/ROMANTIC ELEMENTS

First Publication: JULY 2013

Published by Black Opal Books **http://www.blackopalbooks.com**

DEDICATION

This book is dedicated to Bonnie Hearn Hill, my mentor and friend, who helped me become a fiction author, and to my son Chris Vaughan, who encouraged me to keep writing my own stories.

CHAPTER 1

Cameras flashed around the crew like lightning on an angry sea. Morgan Zeller stepped behind the van to avoid them. Instead, she found Sandi Kapoor talking to a Latina reporter. The reporter was dressed in a black suit jacket and matching slacks despite the murky Florida heat.

Net and cable cameras surrounded Sandi, yet even in her spacesuit, she radiated confidence. Her salt-and-pepper hair, pulled tightly back, contrasted with those hazel eyes of hers, which were so light that they were almost golden.

She placed a hand on Morgan's shoulder and gave the reporter a grin that was more genuine than any of the other astronauts could conjure when dealing with the press. That was only one of the reasons Sandi was their poster child.

"Jamison Robles, this is Morgan Zeller, an astrogeologist who is part of my ground crew," she said. "Morgan discovered an unknown substance in samples returned from the last Mars mission."

If only they could skip this part, Morgan mused. As soon as the astronauts rode off in the van, she could go work at her station in the control room.

A cameraman moved closer to Sandi, next to Jamison. His face wore an expression of unwarranted anger, unlike any Morgan had seen since the day her grandparents died.

"You're a mission specialist on the next crew, aren't you?" Jamison asked her. "I just read your bio."

The cameraman stepped nearer. Again, Morgan flashed back to the day of her grandparents' murder.

"I need to talk to you for a minute," she told Sandi. "Now!"

"We can talk later." Sandi shot her a warning look. *Humor the reporter*, it said, but this was no time to humor anyone.

"I mean it," Morgan said, her voice rising in pitch and volume.

The man took another step, his expression blank now. Mindless.

"No," Morgan yelled and grabbed Sandi's arm.

The silver Astrovan door opened for the crew's traditional ride to their spaceship.

Sandi shook her head. "Let go of me," she said. "You know I've got to leave."

The man jerked the back of his camera open.

"Take cover," Morgan shouted, and pulled Sandi away as hard as she could.

Hot air flashed around them, shoving Morgan off her feet. Amid raining debris, her back slammed the ground. A boom filled her ears, pinning her to the asphalt. Screams drew her into blackness.

ဆဝဆ

Where was Sandi?

Slowly Morgan sat up, her aching back and arms resisting each movement. Her ears rang. Microphones and helmets littered the ground around the Astrovan. A detached hand about two meters away grasped a camera strap. Next to her, Sandi lay in a bloody spacesuit.

"Sandi? Oh, *God.*"

The only answer was a moan. She lay without moving, eyes closed, breathing too quickly. Morgan had to get help.

"What happened?" It was the reporter. What was her name? The sleeve of her jacket was completely torn off, and her arm bore a deep gash. She spoke as if in a daze. "What should we do?"

"Get a doctor," Morgan said. "Right away."

"I'll try." The reporter, whose name she could no longer remember, limped past the van, its wheels stripped of tires.

Sandi's breathing changed to irregular gasps. Lifting her chin to open her airway, Morgan reached for her wrist. A thready pulse beat against her fingers.

All around her people called for help. She couldn't see the reporter anywhere. She reached into her pocket, but her hand shot straight through a hole in the fabric. So much for trying to find her phone.

"Emergency," she yelled, jumping up. "Randy!" Why had she called to him? After that one intimate night together, he was the last person she needed help from. "Koll," she cried out. "Koll, please. We need a doctor over here!"

Ringing filled her ears, the light dimmed, and she lost her balance. As she fell next to Sandi, darkness enveloped her again.

❧❦❧

In a bed at the Kennedy Space Center clinic, Morgan waited to be released. Her head throbbed, and her body still felt sore. A few bandages covered her cuts. The wall clock read fourteen hundred hours, three hours before launch. Why was she still here? Her CT scan had shown only a mild concussion. She had to find out if Sandi was all right and then get to her station before Pax took off. Had they delayed the launch to replace Sandi with Basheer?

"Time for you to get dressed, Zeller."

She looked up into the unreadable face of Timon Brown.

He looked official in his tan summer suit, but he couldn't hide that nervous twitch in his right eye. Not good that the director of the program had time to visit her during the final countdown.

"Didn't mean to startle you."

"You could have knocked." Director or not, he deserved that.

"I tried. You were asleep. And, yes, before you ask, Sandi is going to be fine."

"What about the rest of them? And what happened? An explosion?"

"Unfortunately. A suicide protestor used the old camera-bomb trick. Without your warning, Sandi would have died. Good work."

She shuddered. "The cameraman moved too close to us, and he looked like he was ready to kill someone."

"He managed to kill only himself, but eleven people have serious injuries." Timon looked at his hands, his eye twitching faster. "Unless you're in too much pain, you should get up now. I need you to attend a meeting in two hours."

"But what about the countdown and launch?" She swung her feet over the side of her bed and fought nausea. "How long do we have to delay it?"

"Do you want to go on Pax?"

"Pax Three? Of course, I do." She wasn't ready to stand just yet. "I wanted to discuss the next mission with you, but it can wait."

He put a hand over his eye. "I mean Pax One."

"What? Why?" Panic tightened her throat, making her voice sound higher. "You told me Sandi's all right."

"She's in the hospital, with damage to her internal organs, but thanks to you, she'll recover. We need you to take her place, Zeller. Can you be ready in a week?"

"Just a week?" Chills shot up her spine, but she didn't dare move. This opportunity was at Sandi's expense. Thrilled as she was, she couldn't do more than nod. "Yes, I can be ready."

"The plan is to put her in your slot for the next flight." Timon looked at the clock as Morgan tied the lower string of the gown tightly behind her waist. "Do you agree?"

"Of course," she said. "But I haven't gone through the mission training. What about Basheer? Isn't he Sandi's official backup?"

"He filled that slot only because you were still in basic training on the moon. With his father so ill, he'd rather not leave Earth at this time." He held his palms out, as if welcoming her to the team. "We need you to keep the program going, Zeller. You have more online followers than anyone else at NASA, and after Sandi, you're the top astrogeologist on the planet."

Second in the world? "Who decided that?" she asked.

"Glad to hear you sounding like your old self." He stood and walked to the door. "Be at the Beach House at sixteen hundred to meet with the Pax crew."

She would have answered, would have tried at any rate. But he was already gone.

Her mind raced with training plans. There was no way she could practice even the basic procedures in a week. She'd have to decide which tasks to do now and which ones she could do later on the ship. The mission team was probably making task lists for her already. This was going to be far different than the first mission she had envisioned. Already out of control, it could be a failure if she didn't learn her job fast.

What would the rest of the crew think? They'd spent two years preparing for the trip. Her lack of training would cause resentment. What about Randy? He was supposed to have been a one-night stand, but now, he would be her doctor as they traveled together in a small ship with six other people.

First, she needed to get dressed and let everyone who mattered know she was leaving. She pressed the speaker button on the room phone and then spoke a number as she retrieved her white pants and pale green shirt from the tiny closet. Adrenaline filled her with energy.

"Hello," a cheerful voice answered.

"Mom," she said. "I'm going to Mars."

CHAPTER 2

When Morgan arrived at the Beach House, the first person she saw was Cass. Usually her friend wore a warm, welcoming smile, but today she acknowledged Morgan's arrival with only a slight nod of her braided head. Was she in shock from the bombing?

Flanking Cass, the Pax crew sat around the U-shaped table in the briefing room, with the backup crew in chairs behind them. All of them wore blue sweatpants and T-shirts, and some sported small bandages on their faces and arms, as Morgan did.

Like Cass, everyone looked stunned, as if they were statues with painted faces. They must have just heard that Morgan was replacing her mentor. Knowing she had not trained for a Mars mission, they probably thought her inexperience could put them all in danger. But Morgan had studied every detail of this mission during her free time at the lunar base. If the crew would give her a chance, she could be ready to do the job before they got to Mars.

"Timon and Koll stepped out for a minute," Cass said. She filled the chair with her ample, well-proportioned figure. Black bangs framed her intense blue eyes. "Please sit."

"Thanks." Morgan took the empty chair to her friend's left. Pilot Diego Garcia leaned around Cass and gave Morgan a small wave, which she returned. Across the table, Medical Officer Randall Arnold inclined his head, his blond hair perfectly parted and no expression on his face. She nodded back and blocked the night they had spent together from her mind.

On Randy's right, Mission Specialist Jamese Kim glanced at him. Then she stared at Morgan. "What do you know about this mission?"

"I've read extensively about it and watched all the vids."

Her answer sounded phony. She needed to think before she responded. Her heart pounded. What could she say to this expert electronics engineer who had already been to Mars?

"What do you know?" Jamese repeated.

An engineer would not be thinking about astrogeology, even though the media had run with the PR angle of exploring the planet for evidence of its history. Morgan remembered the vid of Jamese describing her main task for the mission.

"I know you plan to set up electronics and biological systems to support a permanent colony." Her breathing returned to normal. She could always recall everything she had watched or read. Motioning toward Mission Specialist Michelle Dushay, on the other side of Jamese, and astrobiologist Aiden Banks, at the end of the table, she added, "With Michelle and Aiden, of course."

As if the answer had brought them to life, the astronauts around the table shifted in their seats. Some leaned forward and gave all their attention to Morgan.

"My job will be to collect and analyze samples with historical significance," she said. Her bruised muscles tensed in anticipation of more questions.

"How are you going to know what to do with only basic training?" Jamese asked.

"Enough," Timon said, striding into the room in a khaki suit. "Let's allow Morgan some time to get used to being on the crew before we grill her."

Morgan relaxed, grateful for his support. He took a seat at the head of the table. Chief Flight Surgeon Koll Eriksen arrived next, also in a suit. He grinned at her and sat on Timon's right.

She smiled at Koll, whose friendliness helped thaw the chilly reception from her new crewmates.

"We're here to brainstorm about how we can all be ready for takeoff in a week," Timon said, shooting Morgan another grin, "with an astrogeologist who has not had the benefit of the usual training. I regret the violent attack this morning that changed our mission. However, please remember that Morgan thought fast enough to save Sandi's life. I think our new crewmember will do fine."

He pressed a button that lit up the tabletop and then shoved a virtual document toward the center. A copy of the document landed in front of each of them. It was a new schedule. Morgan wondered how the staff had prepared it so fast.

"You haven't had time to process what happened yet," he continued. "But we can't wait. The bombing has caused some legislators to reconsider their support for the Mars program. If we don't leave in seven days, we'll miss this launch period, and the mission might be postponed indefinitely. What can we do to help Morgan take Sandi's place?"

"This doesn't make sense," Jamese said. "Basheer is trained already. Why can't he go?"

"My father is dying," Basheer Rhandavi said from a chair against the wall behind Morgan. His brown eyes looked bleak in his narrow face. "I need to be with him and my family now."

Murmured condolences filled the room.

"The decision has already been made for Morgan to go," Timon said. "We need her expertise, and she has had enough education and training in electronics engineering to assist with the computers throughout the mission."

"Assist me?" Jamese asked, loud enough for a lecture hall, but too loud for a conference room. "She has no training for this mission. We're all going to have to assist her."

"Let me worry about that." Cass patted Morgan's arm. "I can provide any necessary assistance."

"Thanks, Cass," Morgan said, realizing that Jamese would never give her a chance. She would just have to do the best she could to catch up. At least she would have a friend on the journey.

CHAPTER 3

Two days before the rescheduled launch of Pax One, Koll hoped to get a different result from the blood he drew from Morgan's arm for one last test. When he'd seen her go to Randy's room after the party, he didn't know it might be the opportunity he'd been waiting for. Then the explosion changed everything. Unlike Sandi, Morgan wanted to get pregnant. So far her tests had been negative, though. He labeled two vials of blood and then taped the needle puncture on her arm.

She grimaced. "Why did you take so much again?"

"We have to run extra tests just before launch."

"It wouldn't take that much. And why are you drawing blood instead of the lab techs?"

"They're all busy testing. If someone has to redo one, I wouldn't want to interrupt your work to draw more. You're a last-minute addition to the crew, so some of the tests will be run twice."

This was technically true because Koll would run the extra ones. Lying to her made him uncomfortable, but the lies were necessary to get a colony established before the violence on Earth escalated into global war. He had been Morgan's friend since the day she visited NASA four years ago. Her amazing mind was quick enough to keep up with him in intense discussions. They had often talked about the urgent need for colonization of Mars. Terrorists had killed her grandparents. She would understand his deception later.

"Oh, okay." She stood up and stretched as if working out her questions along with her tight muscles. "I'd better get back to the countdown procedures."

He forced himself to return her smile as guilt filled him. "Goodbye, then."

"'Bye," she said on her way out the door.

Koll closed and locked it. He tested half of the blood. The result was positive. Opportunity had finally arrived. If microgravity could help her retain this embryo, as his research had shown it might, he would soon lead a mission of colonists. Would Morgan ever forgive his deceit? At that moment, he didn't care.

He went to his wall refrigerator, pulled out the vial of her blood he had drawn two days ago, and switched the label with the other half of today's sample. Then he set the older blood in a rack for the lab tech to pick up.

A weight of worry lifted from his chest as he put the rest of the fresh blood in the refrigerator. His tenuous plan was coming together years earlier than he expected, maybe in time to save some people from the world's self-destruction. Morgan would need the extra radiation shielding NASA had built into Pax.

He sat at his computer and entered the information about her test into an encrypted file. In a few months, he'd have all the data Congress needed. The senators liked his colonization proposal but wouldn't approve it without more information about pregnancy in space.

Someone knocked on his door. "Dr. Eriksen?"

"Just a minute," he replied, keeping the irritation out of his voice. In a few seconds, he cleared all evidence of the blood test from his counter and hid the equipment in a cabinet. Then he smiled and opened the door.

A woman wearing a white lab coat stood in the hallway. "Hello," she said, extending her hand. "I'm your new assistant, Marcia Reynolds."

"Welcome, Marcia. Nice to meet you." He shook her hand. "I was just preparing a blood sample for the lab." He fetched the vial from his desk and gave it to her. "Would you mind delivering this for me?"

"Not at all," she said. "It's a pleasure to meet you, too." She frowned. "Is this a fresh sample? It seems cold, as if it has been refrigerated."

He stretched his smile wider. "I'm not surprised. The patient complained about my chilly office. I'll turn up the temperature."

"Seems warm enough in here to me. Be right back."

"Take your time," Koll said, but she charged down the hall.

He closed the door and adjusted the wall thermostat so the room would feel cooler when she returned. He had to be more careful until Congress approved his plan.

CHAPTER 4

The centrifuge was first on Morgan's schedule. She ate some whole grain cereal to help prevent the nausea she usually experienced during motion tests. She also drank ginger tea just before she stepped into the centrifuge room.

Jamese motioned to the big chair in the center. She would run the test, with Randy monitoring Morgan's vital signs. Climbing into the chair, Morgan already felt nauseated in anticipation of spinning in circles. She tried not to show her anxiety as she strapped herself down.

After checking the straps, Jamese minced over to the control room in tight sweatpants and stood next to Randy. Her head just reached his chest, and her straight black hair fell halfway down her back.

"Ready?" she asked.

Morgan nodded and wished she had skipped breakfast.

The chair spun slowly at first and then picked up speed on each revolution. Morgan watched the control room go by again and again until it turned into a blur. Half-digested food burned up through her throat and spewed out of her mouth, as if she were a human volcano.

"Noooo," Jamese said.

Morgan closed her eyes. The chair slowed. Then it stopped with a lurch, causing another eruption from her mouth. Her throat burned. Rapid footsteps approached.

Randy grasped her hands. "Are you all right?"

Morgan opened her eyes and looked into his, two pools of green light, offering safety and comfort. She didn't need his help. Reluctantly, she withdrew her hands.

He took a step back.

She unstrapped herself and asked, "Where are the towels?"

"Over here," Jamese said in an angry tone that surprised her.

She had heard that Randy used to date Jamese but was no longer involved with her. From the sound of her voice, maybe she was still involved with him.

Jamese frowned as if Morgan had intentionally wasted her time. "You'll have to complete this test successfully before we can leave."

"I can try again this afternoon."

"Give her some time to recover," Randy said.

"We don't have time to repeat tests."

"I'll do it during my free time this evening." Morgan grabbed a towel. "I can get Basheer to run the test and Koll to monitor it."

"If you don't succeed—"

"We can try again," Randy interrupted. He took another towel and helped Morgan wipe the food from her face and training overalls.

"I need Randy to help me set up your next training exercise." Jamese pressed her full lips together in a pout. "Can you manage without him?"

Morgan looked at him. "Of course, I can."

Randy seemed embarrassed as he followed Jamese to the door. Morgan watched his perfect physique in motion until he left the room. Enough of that. She had to concentrate on her training. While she cleaned up, she visualized going through the procedure for her next exercise, an underwater simulation of freefall.

CHAPTER 5

Buckled into her seat aboard Pax two days later, Morgan fought to control her queasy stomach. The ship rumbled as the engines started. Forcing herself to breathe deeply, she looked for something to focus on. To her right, Randy gripped his armrest while countdown continued over their helmet speakers.

"T minus thirty seconds—T minus twenty seconds—"

She forgot about her nausea. They were taking off. In three months she'd be collecting samples on Mars. The roar of the booster rocket filled her ears.

"Three—Two—One—We have liftoff."

The G force pushed the air out of her chest as if it were a squeeze box. She watched Randy's long, gloved fingers stretch around the end of the armrest. The pressure increased until it seemed to flatten her, stabilizing at three Gs. Her seat rattled. When she thought she couldn't stand the pressure or noise any longer, her vision dimmed. She tried to hang onto consciousness, but light and sound slipped away.

"Are you all right?" Randy asked as she came to.

"I'm fine." She tried to regain coherency before anyone
noticed her lapse. She'd never quite passed out in training.
Must be the excitement of the real trip.

The engine stopped. Suddenly light and free, she watched
the Earth's atmosphere curve slowly by the viewport against
black space. Her crewmates removed their helmets and floated
from their seats like awkward dancers waltzing with the world
below as they reveled in microgravity.

Cass went through her checklist with Mission Control,
resting a hand on Diego's shoulder to stop his somersaults. She
had been to the moon twice as a pilot, and Diego had gone as
her copilot the last time. No one except Morgan knew they
were lovers. If NASA found out, they might be grounded.

Aiden pushed auburn curls away from his face as he
pulled himself along the walls. Like Morgan, he was on his
first mission. She would help him search for evidence of past
life near Columbia Hills.

Jamese took control of the onboard computers from her
workstation. Her straight black hair fanned out and up like
Queen Victoria's ruff. On a Mars mission two years earlier,
she had explored near the Opportunity Rover at Meridian
Planum. Morgan wished she had been there.

Randy floated by to check Jamese's vital signs. She lifted
her eyes to his. If they weren't finished breaking up, it was fine
with Morgan. This was no place for relationship drama.

The French astronaut drifted past. Michelle would set up
closed systems in the surface habitat to prove that a colony
could function continuously on Mars, like the moon bases. At
least Morgan had trained in a lunar habitat, so she would be
familiar with the Martian habitat, which was similar.

Vlad, the Russian engineer, could fix anything, which
made Morgan glad he was on board. He had helped build lunar
bases for his country and the United States, and he'd already

taken two trips to Mars. On the first human mission there, he had revisited the Viking 1 landing site at Chryse Planitia. Then he'd gone with Jamese to Meridian Planum.

Morgan unbuckled her restraints, hooked her boots under her seat, and removed her helmet. Her chest hurt from the takeoff. Orange launch suits swam beneath her head as crewmates moved about. Her stomach cramped, and bits of food sailed from her mouth.

"Grab the vacuums," Cass ordered. "Morgan wins for being first to spout."

Diego retrieved a hand vacuum from its Velcro nest on the ceiling. He chased the contents of Morgan's stomach through the air, between the padded seats, and past workstations. Then he chased Cass while everyone else laughed at his antics.

"Here." Randy handed Morgan a damp cloth, amusement in his eyes. "You should go rest for a few minutes."

"Thanks." She wiped her hot, sticky face, hoping he wouldn't laugh at her. "I'm okay." She pulled a vacuum hose from the wall.

"Would you like some medication?"

A smile dimpled his tanned cheeks. He floated so close to her she could smell the aftershave he wore as an experiment to test its effects on the crew. She didn't want to report how it affected her.

"No, thanks."

Turning away from him, she sipped water from her suit bottle, through a straw beneath her helmet ring, to rinse the bile taste from her mouth. Then she joined the cleanup.

Diego reported the incident of space sickness to Mission Control, amid chuckles coming from the radio. The whole world could hear their conversations.

She replaced the hose and sat at her workstation. The tiny mirror next to the screen reflected her flushed skin. She didn't want anyone to clean up after her again, especially Randy. She started running calculations for the trans-Mars orbit injection.

ᕤᕤᕤ

During their first rest period aboard Pax, Randy knocked on Morgan's door. If she still felt sick, he would offer treatment and then leave as soon as possible, without getting involved.

The door panel slid open. Morgan hovered in black shorts and a lavender T-shirt. Pink toenails tipped her bare feet.

"Randy?"

"I just came by to make sure you are all right." He grabbed the handles on either side of the doorway. Light from the wall screen outlined her blond head and slim waist.

"I'm better. Thanks."

She smiled, and the curve of her lips set off alarms in his head. With Jamese on board, he did not need another complication. Unless she offered food or drink, he could leave in five minutes. But first he should insist that she use her free time to relax.

"Please have a seat." She motioned him in. "There's just enough room for two, with these fold-down chairs and table."

"The table and chairs help provide a feeling of normalcy." He pulled down a chair, floated onto it, and strapped himself in. Information about the ship's computer systems filled half the screen behind her, and messages from her followers on Earth covered the other half. She had not been resting.

She closed the door and buckled herself into the other chair. "You sound like the medical training brochure."

"I wrote it."

"You?" She laughed and pushed her bangs out of her eyes. "That explains all the big words."

He tried not to show that her words stung. "Am I so difficult to understand?"

"No, I'm just teasing," she said. "Would you like some juice?"

"Yes, thank you."

When she unbuckled to reach the wall cooler over the table, he checked the time on his watch. As she took out two bags of apple juice, her breasts were in front of his face. She then shoved a bag toward him with a dazzling smile. He caught the juice while she refastened her buckle.

"Your patient is fine, Dr. Arnold. Any other questions?"

Her deep blue gaze made him shiver inside. "You need to rest more," he said. "Maybe you could watch a movie instead of studying."

"Jamese wants to delegate some tasks to me, so I need to understand how to do them." She pressed a button to turn off the screen. "And it's fun to answer questions from Earth about the mission." She took a sip of her juice, her lips closing into a perfect, tiny circle around the straw. "I'm planning to watch an old movie later, *Raiders of the Lost Ark*. Would you like to join me?"

"I'd like to." The words slipped out before he could stop them. He remembered the touch of her hands on his back and glanced at his watch again. Time to leave. He would not let himself get involved with a coworker again. It was hard enough to be stuck on a mission with Jamese. "Maybe we could watch a movie some other time," he said. "I still have some work to do too."

She unbuckled as fast as he did and drifted with him toward the door. His arm brushed her shoulder, which shocked him like defibrillator paddles. Her face hovered near his. He concentrated on keeping his arms away from her but forgot about his lips. They made contact with her mouth in a kiss that jump-started his heart before he could break away.

When he broke the kiss, her eyes widened in astonishment.

"Good night," he said, and left before he could do more damage.

こ♥こ

The next morning, as Morgan floated toward the wardroom for breakfast, she hoped Randy didn't think anything was different between them. He had acted like he wanted only friendly companionship, but his goodnight kiss had left her quaking inside. This childish reaction was a crush, merely animal lust, brought on by being alone for years. She couldn't allow herself to drift into a relationship that would take time away from the most important work of her life.

She grabbed a handle next to the doorway and paused. The only empty seat was beside Randy. He looked up at her with a smile that reminded her of sunrise on Earth. Trying to smile back professionally, she propelled herself toward the galley next to the table.

In the refrigeration unit, she found some scrambled eggs and toast on a covered plate. She heated them and took a closed cup of the coffee that someone had brewed. Feeling Randy's eyes on her, she put her plate and cup in a magnetic holder and then placed them on the metal table next to him. He turned away and said something to Vlad on his other side as she fastened herself into the empty seat. She hoped nobody had noticed that she and Randy were attracted to each other.

Turning back, he asked her, "How are you feeling today?"

"I'm fine." She started to eat. Their crewmates were discussing their tasks for the day. No one seemed to be watching them closely, so she asked Randy, "What's on your schedule?"

"I need to start some experiments." He looked uncomfortable. "Also, I want to apolo—"

"Maybe later," she said, looking around to see if anyone had heard him. Cass nodded at her from across the table and continued a discussion with Aiden. Morgan nodded back and kept eating.

"Where were you two last night?" Jamese sat at the end of the table on Morgan's right.

"I was in my room." Blood rushed to her cheeks. Afraid that Jamese had seen Randy there, Morgan glanced at him. His face was coloring as well.

"You, too, Randy?" Jamese asked. Everyone else stopped talking and looked at him.

Keeping his eyes on his plate, he scooped eggs into a covered spoon. "I was in the medical bay."

"All night?"

"After finishing my reports, I went to my room and slept. How was your evening?"

"It was okay," she said. "I didn't sleep well, but maybe tonight will be better."

Other conversations resumed, and Morgan finished her meal.

"Excuse me," she said as she left the table, wishing Jamese did not care where Randy had been last night.

❧❧❧

Morgan did not go to the wardroom for lunch, so Randy sent her a message asking if she wanted to talk. She replied, "After dinner."

In the wardroom that evening, Randy lingered at the table while the others finished eating. Morgan sat across from him. He hoped she would stay after everyone else left. He had given her the wrong impression the night before and wanted to correct it. As the medical officer, his responsibilities included the psychological well-being of everyone on board. Without upsetting her, he needed to make sure she understood that they could not have a relationship during the mission, but they could be friends.

"Morgan," he said as soon as they were alone, "I need to apologize for last night."

"Nothing to apologize about," she said with a bright smile.

"I am sorry about the way I said goodnight."

"I'm not," she said. "I enjoyed it."

This was going to be more difficult than he expected. "I did, too," he said. "But we cannot—"

"I know. It would be unprofessional."

"What would be unprofessional?" Jamese asked as she floated back into the room. "I thought I heard voices in here. Mind if I join you?"

"Please do," Morgan said, with no expression on her face.

Trying not to sound irritated, Randy said, "Sure. We are just relaxing here." Jamese's well-being was also his responsibility.

He had always thought of her as a friend, but she had wanted a romantic relationship. They had become physically intimate in spite of his efforts to keep her at a distance, so he had quit spending time alone with her. After all his trouble getting disentangled from Jamese, he did not want another relationship at work. He and Morgan could not go beyond friendship again, at least not until the mission was over.

"What are we talking about?" Jamese asked.

"Friendship," Morgan said and looked at Randy.

Jamese grinned. "Oh, my favorite subject."

"Mine, too," Randy said, wishing he could explain himself to Morgan. Maybe someday it would be different.

"I have a medical question for you, Randy," Jamese said. "It's more psychological, but you've had the basic psychology training."

Morgan sat without moving.

"What is your question?" he asked.

"Do you think it's good for your mental health to spend time alone with a good friend?"

He was not sure what to say. "That's an interesting question. I think it would be healthy for friends to play a good game together. We could turn on the wall screen and find something to play."

"You two go ahead," Morgan said. She unfastened herself from the chair and floated up. "I'm tired." Then she left.

"I'll play with you, Randy," Jamese said in a seductive voice.

He was alone with her. If he didn't play a game with her, she might follow him to his room.

cↄeↄ

As they traveled toward Mars, Morgan and Randy often sat in the wardroom after dinner. They talked, played games, or watched movies there, without any goodnight kisses. She was glad he didn't want intimacy because she had enough trouble controlling her own reactions without worrying about advances from him. Jamese usually joined them, which Randy appeared to tolerate, and her presence helped Morgan maintain control.

Morgan's space sickness returned five weeks after launch, nearly halfway to Mars. During breakfast in the wardroom, she heaved into the air across the table. While the crew cleaned up after her, Randy asked, "Do you want some medication?"

She shook her head back and forth without answering, waiting for the nausea to subside. She wished he wouldn't stand so close, and that everyone would let her clean up after herself.

When her mother had breast cancer, the medicine she took to feel better would cause incapacitating side effects. Morgan did most of the household chores while Mom slowly recovered and Dad worked two jobs. Homework took the rest of Morgan's time, so she seldom went to her high school events or parties. She didn't want anyone to do her work instead of what they wanted to do.

"Maybe you shouldn't eat so much at a time," Jamese said. Her lips looked too full and bright against her small, pale face.

"Yes, please don't," Cass seconded, grinning and chasing a particle with a vacuum hose.

"I'm sorry, everyone, really. I'm fine. It won't happen again." Morgan wanted to suit up and float out into space to be alone for a while. Instead, she went to her room.

There she turned on the wall screen and sent a message.

> *Hi, Koll. I lost my breakfast again, probably because I miss you so much. Please confirm the results of my blood tests. I haven't had a period for more than two months. Your friend always, Morgan.*

She floated to her sleep net in the corner next to her bed to rest while she waited for his reply. Securing herself to the bed seemed like too much trouble. She unzipped the net, climbed in, and zipped it back up. Just as she started to doze off, the screen beeped.

"Alex, read message," she commanded.

In a deep male voice that sounded like Randy's, the computer read the reply from Koll. "Hi, Morgan. Wish I were there with all of you. As you know, you often miss periods, and you had space sickness when you traveled to the moon for your basic training. Are you taking hormones to suppress your cycle? Yours, Koll."

"Alex, send reply," Morgan said. "You know I never take medicine I don't need." Then she said, "Alex, screen off."

෧෨෧෨

A week later, the crew celebrated Cass's birthday at lunch. Cass and Diego held hands under the table, smiling at each other. Morgan wished they wouldn't try to hide their relationship. Everyone in the crew must be aware of it by now.

Diego winked at Morgan, as if he knew what she was thinking. Then he floated up out of his chair and spread his arms to get everyone's attention. "It is time to tell the world how I feel," he said.

"No," Cass said, the smile fading from her face.

Facing her in midair, he assumed a bent-knee position with a flourish and continued, "Cassi, *mi amor*, will you do me the great honor of becoming my wife?"

Cass unbuckled and drifted toward him, above Morgan's head. "Let's go into the other room and talk."

"Uh-oh," Aiden said.

"These are my shipmates and my friends." Diego waved his arms to indicate everyone in the wardroom. "We can talk here."

"OK, but you're not going to like it, *amigo*."

"I like everything about you."

Cass took both of his hands in hers, like a skydiver joining a stunt in midair. "I want to marry you, but not until we retire from off-world missions."

He spun her around in a flat circle while everyone looked up silently from the table, strapped to their chairs. "Why?" he asked, his brown eyes locked on hers.

"When I get married, I want to have children."

"Yes, a big family," Diego agreed with a smile, still turning slowly with her in a flat spin.

"Stop. I can't have children and leave them behind while we go off into space. So ask me again when we have ground duty."

Diego let go of Cass, looked away from her, and said something in Spanish, shaking his head. She returned to her seat, her face expressionless. Then he snapped his fingers, turned a somersault, and said with a grin, "That's a yes, someday. Now it's fiesta time. *Feliz cumpleaños, amante*."

Their crewmembers applauded and shouted, "Happy Birthday."

With a musical giggle, Michelle asked Vlad, "Where's the vodka? I know you brought some on board."

He laughed loudly. "No, I wouldn't do that. Find your own drinks." Then he reached under his chair, pulled out some small plastic bags filled with clear liquid, and passed them around.

"No, thanks," Morgan said. She reached for a second helping of reconstituted stew. "This stuff tastes better the farther we get from Earth."

"Are you all right?" Randy asked in a low voice. "Eating more than usual and then losing it could indicate a serious condition."

She patted his arm. "Take a break from being the doctor. I'm just extra hungry today."

Jamese pursed her large red lips and said, "You were never sick this long in training."

"It's worse now that we're in space," Morgan said, grinning to lighten the mood. She realized that Jamese must have checked all of her NASA records because Morgan had trained only a week for this mission.

"Nothing like the real thing to bring out the worst in you." Aiden raised a bag of vodka and threw his head back. His auburn curls swirled around his face.

"It is unusual to have space sickness this long." Randy's stern look bore through her like a drill. "Examination at fifteen hundred." He pushed off from the table and left.

Her eyes stung with tears, but she blinked them back and looked around the room. The others watched her as if waiting for a reaction. Although her heart sank like a stone, she forced herself to look cheerful. "Have you heard the one about the Martians who landed at the lunar colony..."

❧❧❧

Two hours later, Morgan edged around the fixed table and chairs in the empty wardroom, wondering why Randy had gotten so angry with her. Even with the best remedies he could come up with, ten percent of the astronauts still suffered from space sickness, a few throughout their missions. Some expert. He needed to check his own research.

A little snack would make her less nervous about this exam he insisted on. No one would notice because they were busy elsewhere with afternoon tasks. She took an energy bar from the common cabinet and ate it.

Behind the wardroom a metal ladder led through a crawl space to the medical bay in the ship's central hub. She pulled herself along the ladder and floated past the last few rungs, determined to keep the food down.

When she glided through the doorway of the medical bay, she smiled and said, "Hi, Randy."

"Please lie down," he said without looking at her.

Why was he so unfriendly? She kept her face expressionless as she floated awkwardly onto the table and slipped her feet into the ankle straps.

He took her blood pressure. Then he bent over her chest to listen with his stethoscope. With a frown, he connected the instrument to a machine and slid the scope down to her abdomen. He straightened, moved the ear tips behind his neck, and let the chest piece float out like an accusing finger pointing at her. The skin under his blond hair turned pink.

"When was your last period?" he asked.

She stared at his hands. They gripped the table hard, with white fingers. "About ten weeks ago."

"You're suppressing it with medication?"

"No, but that doesn't mean anything," she said. "You know from my file that my cycle is irregular. I tried to conceive for years but couldn't."

He glared at her. "Well, this time it's a go, unless you have two hearts."

Two heartbeats would mean a child inside her, now, on a spaceship halfway to Mars. How was that possible? Would this be the end of the mission? Had they gone too far to turn around and go back? Randy's face looked fuzzy. The light dimmed.

He shook her gently. "Stay with me," he said. "Explain why you kept your pregnancy a secret."

"I didn't know." She wanted to get away from him and think. Pregnant? How could she be? The fertility procedure had failed, so the baby must be his. Would this ruin his career?

Randy threw his hands up. The sudden movement caused the top of his body to rock back from the table, his feet secured under the bottom rail.

"No, really. The tests before launch were negative."

He grabbed the table edge next to her shoulder and pulled himself in, close to her. "You told me you were infertile. Why were you having such tests done?"

"I had a fertility procedure just before I found out I was going on this mission. Koll Eriksen knew about it."

"You can get a false negative," he said, leaning even closer, until his face almost touched hers.

She nodded and wished he would calm down so she could leave. "I thought so, but Koll said I had no chance of being pregnant. I believed him because the clinic told me I needed surgery first."

"Where are the results of the on-board pregnancy tests you are supposed to perform every month?"

"Koll said I didn't need to bother with them."

"Bother? How could you be so irresponsible?"

Trying not to cry, she realized he was right. She should have performed the tests while there was still time to turn back. "I'm sorry."

"Who's the father?" He moved away suddenly, knocking a nitrous oxide tank off the wall. An alarm buzzed.

"What difference does that make?" She jerked her ankles from the restraints, wiped her eyes, and shoved herself back-ward toward the doorway. Her tears hung in the air as she left.

CHAPTER 6

After a flawless insertion into Mars orbit two months later, Morgan and Cass helped the rest of the crew board the main lander, Cardinal, for their descent to Gusev Crater. Nearly four months into her pregnancy, Morgan had been removed from the landing party because no one knew what a sudden transition to gravity would do to the fetus. She'd read that the baby would be fine in her womb but agreed to stay on Pax to avoid causing another problem. To protect Randy's career, she had not told anyone the baby was his, and he hadn't asked again.

Mars rotated on it axis enticingly below, a red rubber ball just out of her reach. She would never collect rock and core samples there. Jamese would take over her job. Mission Control had cut the time at the planet from sixty days to ten so Morgan could get back to Earth before the baby was born. She had caused the cancellation of many planned experiments and explorations. Although her crewmates had handled the bad news professionally, most of them avoided spending time with her.

She was going to be left behind at what should have been the most exciting time of her life. Yet she would finally have a child, if all went well on the return trip. Full of life but empty of dreams, she wanted to go down and disappear on the vast Martian landscape.

Floating near a window, she watched Cardinal until it shrank to a bright blip and vanished. She should have been on that lander. Tears stung her eyes. She wished the crew a successful landing.

"Ready for final descent," Diego announced over the radio.

"Everything looks good from here," Cass said. "You have a go."

"Copy that," Diego replied. "Descending—looking for a clear spot near the habitat."

Cass reported the start of the final descent to Mission Control and then said to Diego, "Be careful. It's a desert out there."

As he laughed at the old joke, Morgan reminded herself that her problems were insignificant compared to this mission. Koll had said that even with less time for exploration, a successful return after the fast trip and refueling on Mars could speed up the U.S. colonization timetable. While she watched the rusty surface grow closer on the video feed from the lander's cameras, she let her tears fall to relieve the searing regret that she wasn't with the crew. Then she cried with joy that they were landing on Mars at last.

"We're near McCool Hill but have to find a better place to set down, a little farther out," Diego said.

On her screen, Morgan searched for a clearing in the field of boulders. Diego didn't have much time left to land.

"There's one," he said, "Let's try it. Going down slower now. Landing stilts extended. Oh, no!"

The stilts touched sand, and then Morgan's screen went blank. Audio transmission continued with a weak cry for help.

"Diego, what happened?" Cass asked.

"Lander hit rock—fell over—hole under sand—injuries—
" Then the radio went silent except for occasional static.

Moving toward the back of the control room in midair,
Morgan suppressed a surge of dread that made her chest hurt.
She would not panic. The crew needed help. Cass had to pilot
the ship, so she couldn't do much.

Randy was in danger. If she didn't do something, her baby might never know its father. She and Cass might not be
able to get back to Earth without the rest of the crew. She
couldn't just let her crewmates die to keep the baby safe, either. They were all at risk out here. She had to go down and
help them.

Cass was radioing Earth. "Mission Control, this is Pax.
Cardinal fell on its side at landing, approximately half a kilometer from the habitat. The fall injured some or all crewmembers. As you know from the feed, we lost radio contact. Please
advise us. Meanwhile, we're preparing the backup lander for a
possible rescue. Pax out."

"I'll get your suit," Morgan told Cass.

She nodded without taking her eyes off the instrument
panel.

Morgan went to the exercise room, where she collected
the pieces of Cass's landing suit from the cabinet next to the
air lock. Then she brought them back to the control room.

"Cardinal, come in, do you copy?" Cass spoke into the
transmitter. "We're going to help you."

With Morgan's assistance, Cass had most of her suit on
when the message from Mission Control arrived twenty-three
long minutes after her message had started traveling to Earth.

"Pax, follow standard emergency procedures and use your
best judgment. We need more information. How much damage

to Cardinal, and how many injured? Is the air supply intact? Can they get to their suits? Mission Control out."

"Pax here," Cass replied. "Damage and injuries unknown. We have no radio contact. Repeat, no contact." She glanced at Morgan. "We have two sound crewmembers aboard the main ship. Sparrow will be ready for an emergency landing by the time you respond. Pax out." Cass flipped the switches that would activate their two-person lander.

There were too many questions from the ground crew on Earth. Someone needed to do something, fast. Instead of waiting through another transmission delay, Morgan sailed through the doorway and the corridor to the air lock. From the wall cabinet, she retrieved the pieces of her spacesuit and towed them back to the control room. There she removed her sweats and climbed into her thermal undergarment while Cass stared at the lander's instrument readings on one of the screens.

Glancing at Morgan's swollen abdomen under the gray material woven with insulation tubes, Cass asked, "What are you doing?"

"Just being prepared." Maybe she could talk Cass into letting her take Sparrow down. If something else went wrong, Morgan wouldn't have a lander to rescue anyone, and she didn't know how to land the ship. Mission Specialists had minimal pilot training. She would be stranded, alone on Pax until help came from Earth, maybe too late for the baby.

"Pax, this is Mission Control. You need to take supplies to the Cardinal crew in Sparrow, assess any injuries and damage, and get back to us as soon as you know more," the message said, telling Cass and Morgan what they already knew. "The crew can survive on their cabin oxygen for forty-six more hours if the tanks are intact. If not, their suit oxygen should last six days. Take down an inflatable habitat and extra food, water, and medical supplies in case they can't go to the base habitat right away. Good luck. Mission Control out."

"Pax copies you, Mission Control. We loaded the equipment and supplies you described into Sparrow before the first lander left. Going down now. Pax out."

Morgan started to put on her helmet, but Cass said, "What are you doing? I'm going alone."

"You can't." Morgan put her glove on Cass's arm. "We need a pilot on the main ship. You know our last emergency measure is to land Pax. I can't do that."

"How can you manage if you get sick?" Cass asked. "You don't know what the partial gravity will do to you or the baby."

"You're right," Morgan said. "But if I go, we still have a chance to save the crew if the second lander fails. If you go down and can't return, who will take care of the baby and me later?"

"Mission Control isn't going to approve your plan. Orders are for you to stay on Pax. If we land it, we'll all be stranded. You want to have that baby on Mars?"

"Those orders were issued before the lander crashed. If we have to, we could use Pax II as a return ship when it reaches Mars orbit in two months. You know that's why they sent it without a crew, in case we have a major problem. By the time the extra ship arrives, Vlad can fix Cardinal. Please let me go. I have to save Randy and the crew."

"You told me he's just a friend."

"Except for that one night, he is, just like you," Morgan said. She searched Cass's eyes to reach her behind the wide, stern face. "I would go down to rescue you if your lander crashed. You're allowed to use your judgment in an emergency."

Cass blinked. "What if my judgment says you should stay here?"

"Diego's down there too. He might be hurt."

"Oh, go ahead before Mission Control calls back and tells me not to let you. But I should land that little vehicle from here, and you have to come back right after you make sure the crew is all right."

"Okay." Morgan had not thought past the rescue. Of course, she wouldn't be allowed to stay on Mars. Disappointment and regret threatened to overwhelm her, but she repressed her feelings and focused on the task ahead.

"Everything the crew might need is on the sled in Sparrow," Cass said, "You can pull it to them after you adjust to the gravity. Be sure to set the lander for ship pilot so I can control it. I'm going to start streaming all communications to Mission Control as soon as you board. At least we can let them know what we're doing."

೧೨೮೨

During her descent, Morgan searched in the viewer for the other lander. Weak rays from the rising sun lit the landscape orange, like a desert scene through tinted sunglasses. Something fluttered in her abdomen.

"Cass, I just felt the baby move."

"That's exciting," Cass replied over Morgan's suit radio. "Please be extra careful. Have you spotted Cardinal?"

"No, but I see a flash of light to the southeast. Wait, there's a bigger flash west of that. The big one must be Cardinal's reflection."

"Okay. It's still at the last known location. This might get a little bumpy at the end. Will you be all right?"

"Yes. I'm not getting sick the way I did before." She scanned the Martian sands as she came closer and closer to the surface. "There. I see them just before the hills."

"All right. Keep the upper camera pointed at what you saw and the lower camera straight down. I'll bring you in as close to them as I can. When I say to, immediately inflate all the air bags. You and that baby are going to land on the biggest pillow we can make."

"Thanks." Morgan had been worried about using just the parachutes, which could mean a rough landing. The addition of air bags would make the touchdown a lot smoother but less accurate because the lander could bounce in any direction.

"Roger," Cass said. "Starting final descent. Perform landing checks."

"All checks positive," Morgan replied.

"Okay. Here we go."

As the surface rushed toward her, Morgan saw Cardinal pushing up sideways through the sand like the hand of a drowning victim. She kept her gloved fingers near the air-bag buttons and waited for Cass's command. The ground looked as if it would slam into Morgan's lander before she finally heard the command, "Inflate now."

She pressed the buttons and braced herself. Dust flew past the viewports as white bags ballooned over them. The lander bumped, bounced, and rolled around, like a carnival ride. Then it stopped and rocked back and forth. Internal air bags billowed around her. The pull of gravity pressed Morgan into the seat.

"Nice landing," she told Cass.

"Thanks, but you bounced two kilometers away from Cardinal. Good luck."

෴

After unbuckling, Morgan went through the safety checks as she sealed her helmet and the rest of her suit. Cass repeated each checkpoint. Morgan wanted to throw open the hatch and rush out to help Randy and the others, but not following procedures could kill them all.

"Make sure every rope is securely tied on the sled," Cass said from the orbiting Pax.

The sled occupied the seat beside her. Morgan pulled at each knot in the ropes that held down the supplies. "All secure," she replied.

"I'll keep trying to raise Cardinal on the radio while you get started," Cass said. "So far, all I hear is static."

Morgan untied the sled from the seat, opened the air lock, and pushed the sled through to the outer door. She closed the inner door and pushed the button to start the air lock cycle. While she waited for the air to empty and the lock to fill with Martian air, she sipped water from the small plastic tube near her chin. Her suit air had the same antiseptic odor as the lander.

The outer door opened. Climbing outside at last, she lowered the sled to the ground, went down the ladder, and steadied herself on the last rung for a few minutes. Her body didn't feel two-thirds lighter than on Earth. She stretched her left leg and swung it back and forth, then did the same with her right leg. One of the outside video cameras turned toward her. She wished Cass didn't have to film everything for Mission Control.

Morgan let go of the rung and stepped onto the red planet. Excitement tingled through her body and brought the bitter taste of adrenaline to her mouth. Her heart beat faster. On the moon, her first step had been so rushed, in a line of trainees, that she hadn't had time to think about it. She didn't have time to waste now either.

"I'm on the surface," she said into her suit radio, realizing how mundane her first words on Mars would sound to Earth audiences. That didn't matter now. "Any signal from Cardinal yet?"

"Nothing," Cass answered from the orbiting ship. "They landed two-point-zero-five kilometers southeast of you."

Morgan's jelly legs would barely move. Holding onto the lander, she took a few practice steps around it. Then she straightened and turned toward the southeast, where light glinted at the base of the hills.

"I see Cardinal's reflection," she said.

The small sun rose in the reddish sky northeast of the Martian hilltops, which had been named after the crew of the lost Columbia Space Shuttle. Morgan's giant shadow spread behind and to her right across a small, rusty crater.

She pulled the aluminum sled packed with emergency gear and supplies away from the lander. Then she bent over awkwardly to pick up the buckle ends of the yellow ropes attached to the sled.

"I can't fasten the ends of the tow ropes around my waist because they'll slip. I'll just hold them."

"You need to keep your hands free in case *you* slip. Try bringing the ends forward under your arms and buckling them together behind your neck."

"I'll try." Morgan wished she could take off her gloves. After three clumsy attempts, she fastened the ropes together. Then she began trudging through the red oxide sand, fighting to move her feet.

She forced her boots toward the weak reflection of sunlight.

"My belly button is sweating. How can the sun make everything so warm when it's so far away?"

"Your suit will lower its temperature to compensate for the extra blood flow from your pregnancy."

"Oh, that's right."

Walking steadily, Morgan dragged the sled over the uneven terrain of Gusev Crater. Soon she stopped sweating. The sled rose, dipped, and bumped, leaving a dark scar across the burnt-umber ground. She longed to lie down in the alien, rock-strewn soil and read the history of this world.

Morgan knew the area well from data returned by the Spirit Rover and unmanned orbiters. The grandeur of the real landscape stunned her. The ancient impact crater, ninety miles from rim to rim, could hold Oregon's Crater Lake ten times. Overlaying craters scalloped the rusty edges of Gusev. She could just make out where the Ma'adim Vallis channel had once entered the basin from the south, when the ancient water flowed. Now smaller craters pockmarked the dry lakebed.

She passed serpentine drifts of red oxide sand, dotted with small gray rocks. Large boulders, scoured by lava and ice, dug into the russet sediment. They cast shadows that looked like broken fortune cookies.

Toward Gusev's southeast edge, the Columbia Hills rose in round, red-orange peaks like scoops of ice cream in a flavor Morgan had never tasted. Morning frost still streaked the mounds like white coconut strands. Low in the pink Martian sky to the east, the distant sun warmed the soil, sublimating the frost into wispy strands of mist.

"Oh, Cass, I really wish you were here."

"No, you don't," she said. "I'd have to ground my spectacular ion ship to get there. Now move. You don't have time for sightseeing."

After the sudden change from microgravity, Morgan's body adjusted quickly to the low Martian gravity. Walking was difficult but possible. Stretching her legs across the sand was more satisfying than walking the treadmill on the ship. *Just keep moving one foot after the other*, she told herself. She could do this. The sled wasn't too heavy for her to pull here.

Floods spreading north to the Elysium basin had eroded the western rim of Gusev Crater. Layered bedrock recorded the wet history of sulfur, bromine, and chlorine beneath volcanic boulders on the rough, magenta plains. Goethite still held a fraction of the centuries-old moisture in carbonated stones.

She placed each boot carefully between volcanic rocks, tugged the sled through oxidized soil, and worried about her baby. Could forcing herself to step and pull so much cause a miscarriage? No. Her exercises aboard ship had prepared her for such activity. This must be all right.

As if in answer, a butterfly moved inside her. Grateful to feel life, she slowed her steps, hoping a few extra minutes wouldn't cause the Cardinal crew any additional suffering. She just needed to go a little slower and breathe evenly. The baby would be fine rocking in its bed of amniotic fluid, as long as she didn't overdo it. She had read that pregnant women could continue their normal activities into the last trimester, and she had trained to walk on Mars.

"Cardinal, this is Morgan. Come in, Cardinal." They still weren't sending, but just in case they could receive, she added, "I should arrive within fifteen minutes."

The low gravity helped lengthen her steps as she strode toward Columbia Hills, passing rocky outcrops that held secrets of ancient days. The hills grew larger. She spotted Cardinal lying hatch down near West Spur, half-buried in the sand, like a big, tipped-over water tank. Two of its metal legs stuck out uselessly into the air.

"Cardinal is on its side, Cass, hatch down. Sandy soil covers about half of it."

"Oh, no. You'll have to dig them out. I should have gone down there."

"Don't worry. I can do it." Morgan sighed. "I just wish we knew if everyone is all right."

Something moved behind one of the lander's viewports. Her muscles went limp with relief.

She waved at the port. "Hello, I'm here."

Two faces crowded the round window and grinned.

"Diego and Randy are looking through the aft viewport," she all but shouted.

"Yippee," Cass yelled.

Then Morgan unbuckled the sled ropes, dropped them, and ran in flying leaps the final few meters to the window. Diego pointed at his ears, nodded yes, and then covered his mouth and shook his head.

"They can hear our transmissions but can't send any," Morgan told Cass. "They already know what we're planning to do."

Randy pointed to her belly with a question in his eyes.

"We're both fine, Randy, just tired. Don't worry. Didn't you tell me exercise is good for an expectant mother? How is everyone on Cardinal?"

He held up four fingers and smiled. Then he held up two fingers, frowned, and moved away from the port. Aiden and Jamese appeared in the window.

"Four Cardinal crewmembers are all right," she reported to Cass, "but I think Vlad and Michelle are injured."

Aiden nodded.

"Start digging," Cass said. "But don't rush. They should have plenty of air left."

"It shouldn't take more than a couple of hours. I'll check on the crew often."

Aiden made funny faces and waved behind the window.

Morgan laughed and waved back at him. Then she retrieved the sled, unpacked a shovel, and started to dig sand away from under the lander. Careful not to hit the smooth hull or her suit, she filled the shovel and then threw the contents behind her, over her left shoulder. Wanting to examine every grain of sand, she wouldn't let herself think about the information in the ground she was moving. Each time she removed a shovel full, half as much dirt drained back in from the sides. After ten minutes, she was still two meters from the hatch. Then she dug enough sand out to get half a meter closer.

Her arms ached, so she dropped the shovel and stretched them. She leaned out but couldn't see the port. A return of the nausea made her light-headed, as if she were back in microgravity for a few seconds. She wished she could have a normal pregnancy, doing everything right instead of just hoping that her actions weren't endangering the baby. She should have refused to come on this mission, but if she had, she might not be pregnant. According to Koll, the microgravity had probably kept her from miscarrying again.

"Tired," she said. "Resting now." Gasping for air, she sat on the sled and concentrated on breathing in through her nose and out through her mouth. She drank water through her helmet tube and took slower breaths.

When her breathing returned to normal, she got up, stepped around to the viewport, and asked, "Are you guys okay?"

Diego held up a sign: *Air leaking. Two hours left. Can't reach suits. Vlad unconscious.*

Her heart skipped. "Was the tank punctured?"

He nodded and held up another sign: *Air lock controls damaged. Need door unlatched to get suits.*

"Morgan, what's going on?" Cass asked. "What tank? You're supposed to be taking a break, but your heart rate and blood pressure just increased."

"Cardinal has an oxygen leak, with only two hours of air left. Vlad is unconscious. The crew can't reach their suits in the air lock until I unlatch the inner door manually."

"You need to come back and let me go down there. Your vitals keep changing. If your nausea gets worse, you could re-gurgitate something into your air supply and—"

"I know the risks. The digging will take longer than I cal-culated, at least an extra half hour."

Aiden and Jamese reappeared in the window. He looked scared. She glared at Morgan as if blaming her for their plight.

"Morgan, I have to give you this message from Mission Control," Cass said in an odd, stilted voice. "They're glad you have some good news, but they want you to leave the emer-gency supplies, return to the ship, and let me go down."

In the window, Aiden looked shocked, as if someone had punched him in the stomach. Jamese's face twisted in rage. They could do the math in their heads. The oxygen wouldn't last for everyone. Mission Control had asked if they could get to their suits but hadn't waited for an answer before sending the message. The government would rather make martyrs of the trapped astronauts than risk the bad publicity if Morgan's baby didn't survive.

Morgan had no choice. Her shipmates needed help. She couldn't let any of them die to save her baby or herself. "They won't all live until you get here," she told Cass.

"You need them to get you back home before the baby is born," Cass said.

"Yes, we both need them. Not that it matters, but did Mis-sion Control order me back?"

"No. It's still up to me."

"Okay," Morgan said. "As soon as I clear the hatch and unlock the door so the Cardinal crew can take over, I'll start back."

"Good girl."

ↄ⌐ↄↄ

Grimly ignoring her exhaustion, Morgan dug steadily for the next half hour. Bent over, she scraped sand into the shovel from a deepening hole and tossed it to her right side because her left shoulder hurt.

She went to check on the crew again. The window framed Vlad and Randy's smiling faces, a sight that energized her.

"Vlad is alert and okay now," Morgan reported to Cass.

Randy motioned for Morgan to rest. She shook her head and went back to digging. The baby had her oxygen, but Randy's was running out. He would be first to give up his air so someone else could survive.

She stretched out on her left side under the lander to maximize the flow of blood to the baby while she removed more sand. Forcing herself to breathe slowly, she filled the shovel, ladled the sand out, and spilled it just far enough away so it wouldn't fall back in. Her skin itched with sweat, and she hurt all over. She turned down her suit temperature on the arm control. Then she repeated the filling and dumping motions until the hole was deep enough for a person in a spacesuit to crawl out.

"Diego, I'm going to open the hatch now," she said. "Empty the air lock."

While she waited for the air to cycle, she checked the time on her arm readout and felt faint again. There was just enough time to unlatch the door and recycle the air lock again before they ran out of air. She needed to rest before starting back but couldn't take a break until the crew could get to their suit tanks. When the outside gauge read empty, she unlocked the hatch, went through the outer air lock door, and closed it behind her. She pressed a button to refill the compartment with air and retrieved the tool to open the inner door manually from the wall. As soon as the inside gauge read full, she used the tool to unlock the inner door. Her arms burned.

"Your air lock will open from the inside now," she told the crew. "Wait until I get out of your way and the lock fills with air."

She repeated the air cycling procedure in reverse and secured the hatch. Soon the outside gauge read full. They had ten minutes of air left to get into their spacesuits.

"Cardinal crew, you're good to go outside."

"Great job, Morgan," Cass said. "You need to rest now. I'll be out of communications range, on the far side of the planet, soon."

"I have to crawl backward through the hole first so they can get out."

"Okay, but be careful."

Morgan backed out slowly. She moved her left knee back and then her right until she reached the edge of the hole. To protect the baby, she kept her abdomen off the ground and used her arms and knees to shove her herself back over the edge to scoot out.

CHAPTER 7

Randy rushed ahead of Jamese to open the Cardinal hatch, anxious to see if Morgan was all right. She had stopped talking to them, and Cassandra was out of range.

"I'm supposed to go first," Jamese said through her helmet radio.

He put his boot through the hatch. Jamese slid hers out to block his other foot.

"This is a medical emergency," he said. "Move."

"You can't just say that and change our protocol." Her boot remained in his way.

He tried to push Jamese back. "Any delay could kill Morgan or the baby."

She ducked below his arm.

"Jamese," Diego said, "As ground commander, I order you to stand back."

"No. You have to follow the mission directives."

Vlad stood up behind her. "My hand is on your air valve, Jamese. Okay, Diego?"

"Wait," she said and then withdrew into the ship. "You'll face charges for that, Vlad."

"Not according to regulations," Diego told her. "We'll talk later."

Already partway through the hole Morgan had dug under the hatch, Randy could not focus on the argument. Until he knew that she was still alive, no one else existed for him. Time stopped as he crawled in his spacesuit to the side of the hole. At last he pulled himself up and out from under Cardinal and staggered to his feet. He stood on the surface of Mars again, beneath a poisonous sky and tiny sun.

The woman he loved, who had given them oxygen just in time, lay sprawled on her back next to a pile of rusty Martian soil she had dug out. Her spacesuit and helmet looked intact.

He knelt by her side. Her eyes were closed, mouth open. The electronic display on her right sleeve showed a normal heart rate but only ninety-two percent pulse oxygen.

"Morgan, can you hear me?" he asked through his suit radio.

No response.

Diego leaned over him. "What can I do?"

"Help get her inside, and bring me two air tanks from the sled," Randy said. "She needs an oxygen mask to prevent hypoxia in the fetus."

"Good plan. After that, I'll take the rest of the crew to the habitat and then come back for you."

With Diego's help, Randy turned Morgan onto her left side to increase blood flow to the placenta. Her skin color appeared normal. She took shallow, rapid breaths.

"Vlad, please stay in the lander," Randy said. "We need your help, and you need more time to recover from your concussion."

"Will do," Vlad said over the radio.

"Everyone else hurry out," Diego said. "We need to take Morgan back through."

"She's still breathing, so she must be all right," Jamese said as she stood next to Randy. "Pregnant women faint a lot."

Anger flashed through him. He shot her a warning look.

She kept talking. "Cass should have come instead. We need to get to the habitat."

He needed to focus on his patient. He stood and reached under Morgan's arms to lift her. Diego picked up her legs. Randy struggled with the extra suit weight in the unfamiliar gravity as he backed into the hole. He pulled her head and shoulders after him while Diego pushed against her boots. At the hatch, Vlad pulled Randy in until they got Morgan inside.

They settled her into the back right seat, where she would have ridden if she had descended with them. Randy reclined the seat and put her footrest up.

Diego brought the first oxygen tank to Vlad.

"We can't spare more than one tank," Jamese said. "We could have a problem on the way to the habitat."

"You have six days of air in your suit."

Diego set the additional oxygen inside the hatch and left. Vlad connected the tank to the ship's air supply, sealed the hatch, and cycled the air lock.

"Good job, people," Randy said to the crew outside through his suit radio. He watched Morgan's breathing, impatient to take her helmet off. "Thank you. Diego can bring back a rover to transport Morgan and Vlad."

"We can't just send a rover," Jamese said.

Randy's anger flared again, but he forced himself to remain calm, his eyes on Morgan's parted lips. He had to wait until the cabin pressurized to treat her.

"Why not?" It was Diego's voice. He could handle Jamese.

"Because the rovers have been sitting there since the supply ship dropped them, and regulations require us to run tests before we can drive one."

"*Madre mía*," Diego said. "Those regulations don't apply in an emergency, Jamese. Catch up, or we'll leave you out here alone. The habitat is half a kilometer away."

"We could walk faster without her," Aiden said. "She has the shortest legs."

"I'm coming," Jamese said. "But this will all go in my report to Mission Control."

"Good," Diego said. "Then I won't have to report it. You pull the supply sled."

The radio went quiet. Relieved, Randy concentrated on Morgan. As soon as the air and pressure gauges read normal, he and Vlad took off their gloves and helmets. Then they removed her spacesuit.

She looked fragile in her thermal undergarment, which stretched over her rounded abdomen where her baby grew. Was it his baby, too?

Randy pulled on sterile gloves and then listened to her heart and lungs with his stethoscope. They sounded normal, but she still strained to breathe, as if her airway were partially blocked. He performed a quick chin lift and finger sweep, which cleared a bit of food. She coughed. He retrieved a nasal cannula from his bag.

"Vlad, I need the other tank."

"Sure." Vlad placed it next to her seat.

"Thanks." Randy attached the tube to the tank, adjusted the oxygen, and put the cannula in Morgan's nostrils. Still not awake, she started taking normal breaths.

Her pulse oxygen soon rose to ninety-eight percent. He checked her heart and lungs again and then moved the stethoscope lower.

The fetus's heartbeat sounded strong. After they returned Morgan to Pax, Cassandra could run some tests in the medical bay for him.

Randy shivered. For now he could only wait beside his unconscious, pregnant patient in a crashed spaceship on a hostile world.

CHAPTER 8

Morgan woke up inside a crew module, reclined in a flight chair, without her spacesuit. She must be in Cardinal. Was everyone okay?

Her throat hurt, and someone had put oxygen tubes in her nose. Her thermal undergarment felt damp and sticky. She removed the tubes, stood, and wondered how she could get back to Pax. Sitting next to her without his helmet, Vlad smiled and motioned for her to lie down again.

"You're okay," she said. "Is everyone else?"

He nodded.

Relief coursed through her. "I need to get back to Pax. Where are the rest of the crewmembers?"

"They went to the ground habitat," Randy said from behind her. "You need to put the cannula back in and rest."

She turned toward him. He sat at a terminal in his spacesuit and headgear, tapping a keyboard.

"What happened?" She cradled her abdomen. "Is the baby all right?"

"Yes, the fetus is fine." He swiveled his chair to face her. "As soon as you finished rescuing us, a bit of food lodged in your airway. Please take deep breaths."

She concentrated on breathing in and out and then asked, "How can I get back?"

"Diego will return soon with a rover. When he arrives, Vlad will get you ready for transport." Randy's eyes moistened like dew on grass. "Thank you for saving our lives."

"Yes, thank you, Morgan," Vlad said, with a flourish of his hand from his heart toward her. "My deepest thanks for your courageous action. If you ever need anything, just ask me."

Morgan wasn't sure what to say, so she smiled at each of them, sat on her reclined seat, and put the tubes back into her nose. Her body hurt all over, as if she had overdone a workout.

Randy handed her a bag of orange juice. She sipped the sweet liquid.

"I'm supposed to go right back to orbit," she said.

"Yes, we heard the transmission," Randy said. "Cassandra has enough medical training to take care of you when you get to Pax. She can always contact me for help." He hesitated, looking deep into Morgan's eyes the way he used to. "I am sorry you have to go back up, but you will be safer and more comfortable there."

Morgan wished she could get back without his help. "I'm sorry that everyone has less time on the surface."

He didn't respond.

The air lock recycled. Morgan turned to the door. A spacesuited figure entered, short, with green sleeve stripes. Diego removed his helmet.

"It's good to see you awake, *amiga*," he said.

"Thanks." She felt like a bad child being sent home from school. No matter how difficult it was to leave, she wanted to go back quickly and get out of their way. Then they could do at least some of the work that thousands of people had planned for years.

"Are you two slackers ready to take a ride?" he asked the men.

"As soon as we get dressed," Randy replied. "Would you mind helping Morgan suit up?"

"I can manage," she said, but when she stood up, her feet felt heavy. Diego helped her put on her spacesuit, and Vlad sealed her helmet and gloves. She went through the safety checks with him and then started out the hatch.

Randy's baritone voice filled her helmet. "If you feel the slightest nausea, please let us know immediately."

He walked right behind her, so she just nodded because talking made her throat worse. He helped her climb into the back seat of the rover and fastened the seat belt over her bulky suit.

"I will be right back after I stow my gear in back," he said. "Diego, can we fill the cabin with air in case I need to take off her helmet quickly?"

"*Si, si,*" Diego replied.

Randy climbed into the seat on her left while Diego took the wheel and Vlad sat in front. Diego drove the rover's huge tires back over the Martian terrain that she had crossed on her trek from the emergency lander. It still stood two and a half kilometers northwest of Husband Hill. Again, she had no time to stop and explore, and now she never would.

The dizziness started again. "I'm sick," she said.

"Breathe in and out slowly." Randy said as he took her wrist in his glove and checked her forearm display. "If you feel worse, we can stop and set up a portable habitat."

She shook her head. Suppressing her disappointment at leaving so soon, she concentrated on breathing so she wouldn't delay them from their work anymore than necessary. She would have plenty of time to feel sorry for herself aboard Pax while her crewmates did her tasks.

eɔeɔ

Still very sore when the rover stopped, Morgan had to lean on Randy's arm to get to the lander and take her seat inside. She hoped they could take off quickly.

Diego started going through a checklist over the lander radio with Cass. Randy and Vlad waited outside the open hatch. She didn't like them watching her being sent away from Mars. Why didn't they just get in the rover and go? Finally, Diego waved, ready to take off. To be polite, Morgan also waved and said goodbye. She didn't want to talk to anyone, especially not Randy. Her cheeks burned with embarrassment.

While Diego secured the door, she fastened her shoulder belt. "Ignition," he said.

No noise or vibrations came from the engine.

"Try again," Cass said over the radio.

Diego tried, but the engine didn't turn on.

"I'll start it from here," Cass said.

Nothing happened.

"Damn. The readout says the engine is damaged." Cass almost never swore.

Uneasiness took hold of Morgan. She forced herself to stay calm for the life inside her.

"It doesn't say where the damage is," Diego said.

"I'll find out what's wrong," Vlad said, his voice coming through Morgan's suit receiver.

Pounding noises started coming from the hull. Why couldn't this be over, her ignominious dismissal from the planet that she had dreamed of exploring? At least she would hold the record for the shortest stay on Mars. She should have already been back on Pax.

"Are you all right?" Randy asked over the radio.

"Yes, Diego's taking good care of me," she said. Diego patted her shoulder.

"Forget the engine," Vlad said. "A small meteor punched a hole in the protective covering. The dust got in and ruined some of the parts, so none of us can go back yet. Neither lander can take off without repairs."

His report stunned Morgan. Her friend, orbiting alone, must be devastated by the news.

"You mean we might have to land Pax?" Diego asked, putting words to Morgan's anguish.

"Yes," Vlad replied. "If we can't get a lander working, we might have to get parts from Pax, or make them on the ship."

"Then we would have sixty days to repair the landers and get into orbit before the extra return ship arrives," Diego said, his voice too cheerful. "We wouldn't have to shorten the mission."

Cass didn't say anything over the radio. Anger usually made her quiet. Diego wasn't attached to Pax the way she was.

Morgan closed her eyes. They'd gone over the emergency procedures in her short training the week before launch, but no one had thought a double lander failure would ever happen. Now they might lose Pax. If the big ship landed, they had no way to launch it again from the rocky Martian soil. Their Pax, which had brought them to a fascinating other world, would become a relic for people to visit on future trips. Sadness for Cass overwhelmed her. She cried silently, her tears running into the saliva trap at the base of her helmet.

"We need to get Morgan to the habitat." Randy's voice crackled through her receiver.

So she might stay after all, at the cost of her best friend's magnificent ship, the highest achievement of the space program. If Cass had brought the lander down, it might still be functioning. Morgan should not have insisted on rescuing the crew herself.

๛๛๛

As they neared the base of McCool Hill in the rover, Morgan spotted the power plant with its tall storage tanks. It had been steadily producing fuel and water for eighteen months. The continual operation on Mars of something made by humans cheered her. She would do everything she could to keep her baby safe here and work hard for the mission. Randy didn't act interested in continuing their friendship. If she could just be accepted as part of the crew again, though, and do her job, that would be enough for now.

By the time their rover pulled up next to the uncovered one in front of the habitat, she felt almost normal. Her training, even though short, had prepared her for living on Mars. Small cylinders encircled the large metal cylinder they would stay in. It stood one hundred meters southwest of the power plant. The inflated lab rested on the other side of the rovers. No greenhouse had been erected because they weren't planning to stay long enough to grow crops. Prepackaged meals would sustain them, unless they had to extend their visit. Morgan's heart pounded. Her baby could be born here.

"Take my arm," Randy said as he jumped to the ground.

"I'm much better, thanks," she said. "I can manage." She got out of the rover without assistance and entered the habitat. The air lock opened into the exercise room, just like on Pax. The habitat duplicated the Pax crew quarters, but with less room to move around because they could walk only on the floor. She removed her suit and stowed it in the cleaning chamber.

Michelle, Aiden, and Jamese bounced in through the internal doorway, filling the room. It was designed for two people at a time to exercise or suit up.

"How are you?" Michelle asked. "We were so worried." She grabbed Morgan's right hand in hers. A sling held Michelle's left arm.

Aiden hugged Morgan and said, "Thanks for coming to the rescue. I knew you'd be all right."

"I'm still really tired." Morgan enjoyed the renewed companionship that had been missing for weeks. "Where can I stay tonight?"

"Same room as on Pax," Michelle said. "But you need some food first. Come on."

Morgan followed Michelle down the hall to the wardroom, which had a table and chairs identical to the ones on Pax, except that they weren't bolted down. Soon everyone sat at the table, thanking Morgan. Maybe she could resume her place among them.

❧❧❧

After a reconstituted meal, Morgan asked Randy, "Do you have time to check the baby's heartbeat?"

"Yes," he said. "Please come to the medical bay."

She said good night to the others and then climbed the ladder in the corner of the room. He followed silently. Instead of floating to the exam room, as she did on Pax, she had to move on her hands and knees through the crawl space, which tired her. He bumped into her foot.

"Sorry," he said.

"No problem."

She crawled faster, but exhaustion set in when she reached the corridor. Although she tried not to show how much she ached all over, he took hold of her left elbow and supported her the rest of the way.

He helped her onto the exam table. Then he listened to her abdomen with his stethoscope.

"The baby's heartbeat sounds fine," he said, with a gentle smile that she wanted to kiss.

Instead, she smiled back. "Now I can sleep."

෴

He took her to her room and waited until she opened the door. Although the room had never been occupied, it had bedding as well as a standard entertainment system on the wall. The setup was the same as on Pax, but everything had changed so much since the first time he had visited her room.

Randy lingered in the doorway. "Good night, Morgan."

She reached toward the refreshment cabinet.

"Would you like—"

He kissed her on the forehead. "You need to rest."

That small kiss sent a thrill of pleasure through her. After he closed the door, she wondered if they were friends again. Maybe so, but she couldn't worry about that now. Her baby's survival depended on how well she took care of herself. Also, she had work to do here if she could do it without any additional risk to her child.

෴

The next day, their second on Mars, Randy climbed behind the wheel of an uncovered rover. He and four others split into two teams to attempt lander repairs. He had left Morgan in the habitat to rest, with Michelle to help her and a radio handy to contact him or Cassandra.

Jamese buckled her seat belt next to Randy. He hoped they would not have a problem with her today as he pushed the button to pressurize the cabin. When the green light flashed, he removed his helmet and handed it between the seats to Diego, who sat behind Jamese.

"Diego, do you think we can use the rovers to pull Cardinal upright?" Randy asked. He started the motor.

"Maybe, but first we have to assess the damage."

"While you do that," Jamese said, smiling brightly, "I'll pack everything we can use into the rover."

She was trying to take control again already. Randy knew he might have to intervene to back up Diego's authority.

As the rover pulled away from the habitat, Diego said, "All of us should do damage assessment."

Randy headed north toward Cardinal, across the brick-red sand. He waved at Vlad, who was turning the other rover northwest

"I think that's a waste of time," Jamese said. "We're already late doing our scheduled tasks, with Morgan's work to do also."

Irritated with Jamese's suggestions, Randy reminded himself that she had a right to express her opinions. Without taking his eyes off the rock-littered course ahead, he asked, "Could we please just get the lander working today?"

"Last time we were here, we never let ourselves get behind schedule," she said. "No matter what happened."

His temple started to throb. He drove between a pair of dark gray rocks that stood like sentinels guarding a crater the size of a backyard swimming pool. The rover bumped over the uneven ground.

"You didn't have two landers broken down," Diego said. "Right now, we need to find out what's wrong with Cardinal."

"Doing unscheduled tasks eliminates the tasks we planned for our mission," Jamese said. "We spent two years planning, and we should stick to our plan."

A dull pain settled into Randy's forehead. He wanted to enjoy the panorama of the Columbia Hills to his right, which rose from the florid soil as the rover rolled toward West Spur. The small sun lit a pale apricot sky, casting the rover's shadow to his left. On the right, Husband Hill went by.

"Why can't we just land Pax and fix the landers slowly, in our spare time?" Jamese asked.

"Pax would provide better protection for Morgan in space," Diego explained. In the rearview mirror, Diego's suited arms made small circles as he spoke. "We can run the plasma engine to generate a magnetic field around the ship to shield her from radiation."

"Did we come all this way to have our activities revolve around Morgan?" Jamese asked. "Her surprise already cost us six weeks, but landing Pax would give us that time back because we'd have to wait for the extra ship. We could dig a big hole here and put her in it to protect her from radiation."

"Jamese, I do not want to hear any more complaints about Morgan," Randy snapped. "She saved our lives."

"Cassandra could have done that," Jamese said, her voice low.

"We want to keep Pax in orbit, if possible," Diego said. "So we don't have to use our last backup system. We should try to save the extra ship for the next mission."

Randy's head pounded by the time he finally caught a glimpse of Cardinal, which reflected the dim sunlight. "We're here. Can we work together on this, please?" He parked the rover next to Cardinal.

"All right," Jamese finally agreed. She put on her helmet. "I just want us to make the best use of our reduced time on the planet."

As soon as the cabin depressurized, Randy followed Diego into the hole beneath the lander, wishing Jamese were not with them.

e⁄ɔe⁄ɔ

A few hours later, Randy steeled himself for more trouble as he drove the rover back. He needed to find a way to gain Jamese's cooperation. Diego transmitted the bad news to Cassandra, Mission Control, and everyone on the ground.

"Cardinal has sustained too much damage to fly without extensive repairs. The spare parts are ruined, too. To fix the main lander, we need to pirate some parts from Pax."

At the other lander site, Vlad replied, "We also need more parts."

Randy knew Mission Control would order Cassandra to land Pax. He had heard her say only a handful of words all day, just acknowledgements of messages. Diego looked worried.

"Why can't Cassandra just send down the parts?" Jamese asked.

Not again. Why did she have to question every decision? Frustration filled Randy, like it used to when they were dating. She tried to be in charge of every situation. If Mission Control wanted her input before making the decision, they would have asked. Still, as part of the team, she had a right to give input. Maybe his reactions to her, based on their history together, were part of the problem. He decided he would try to be more patient.

Diego answered Jamese's question like a teacher speaking to a class of fifth graders. "If the parts landed too far away, we couldn't get to them in a rover. You know that we would need to get back to the habitat before the temperature drop at sundown."

"Can't Cassandra calculate where to send the parts within our excursion limits?" Jamese persisted. "She managed to land Morgan within walking distance."

"Apparently Morgan made the right decision to come down herself," Randy said, not bothering to keep annoyance out of his voice. No matter what he said or did, Jamese would always push it too far. "If she had not, Pax would have no pilot now to land it, and we could all be stranded."

"I guess so," Jamese said. "Still, she could wait for the next ship and bring down a lander from it."

"And what if that lander crashed?" Diego asked. "And what if the hydroponics system doesn't work well enough to feed us that long?"

She didn't speak the rest of the way back, for which Randy was grateful. The less interaction with her, the better. His back ached from moving supplies and equipment from Cardinal to the rover, and he needed to concentrate on avoiding boulders. Also, he wanted to watch the alien landscape roll by in waves of rusty sand peppered with gray rocks.

ϾྜϾྜ

Morgan waited for the returning rover teams in the wardroom, dressed in an oversized blue T-shirt and gray sweats that stretched across her expanding waist. She wanted to go somewhere where the crew wouldn't have to see her again. Rather than hide, though, she would face everyone at once and discuss the revised mission professionally.

Michelle sipped juice with her at the table, apparently lost in thought.

When the others came in, no one appeared to be upset with Morgan except Jamese, who glared at her. Morgan had expected irritation from Jamese over the changes in their plans, but not anger. Did she still blame Morgan for throwing them off schedule? That didn't quite explain Jamese's attitude now that they would stay the entire sixty days after all.

While everyone found a seat for dinner, Morgan asked, "When is Cass coming down?"

"Just after dawn here tomorrow," Diego said. "How are you feeling?"

"I'm almost fully recovered," Morgan said. Randy's eyes examined her. "Another night's sleep should do it," she added. "Thanks, everyone, for rescuing me after I fainted."

"*De nada*," Diego said. Others chimed in with, "You're welcome."

To clear the air with Jamese, who sat next to her, Morgan said, "Tomorrow I'm going to ask Mission Control to restore me to active duty."

Chewing a mouthful of food, Randy nodded his approval.

"That's good to hear," Jamese said. "We're already a day behind, and we have to unload Pax now and fix the landers. Even without taking on your work, we probably need to cancel some of the exploration and tests we planned."

"Does anyone else feel that way?" Morgan asked.

The others shook their heads or said "no" or "not me."

"Morgan, I haven't forgotten that you saved our lives," Randy said while staring at Jamese.

"Let's drink to that," Vlad said. He passed out a round of bags filled with clear liquid and gave Morgan apple juice.

Wondering how Vlad had managed to smuggle so much vodka from Earth, she said, "We're all welcome for saving each other."

"Here's to Morgan," Aiden said. He threw back his wild, curly hair and took a long drink. Everyone except Jamese joined in. She returned her bag to Vlad's supply under the table, which only Morgan seemed to notice. Something else must be bothering Jamese.

CHAPTER 9

The next morning Diego suited up with his crewmates at dawn to watch Cassi come down from orbit. He took the wheel of the uncovered rover, and Jamese took the covered one, as everyone climbed in. Leading the way out of the hills, Diego drove across wavy sand. The coarse, rock-littered soil reminded him of a yard filled with valuable car parts left out to rust in the weather. He stopped near Lahontan Crater and waited to retrieve his beloved.

Diego's heart pounded too fast. So many things could go wrong with the descent. They had already wrecked both landers. He tried to think only of Cassi's smiling face so he could push the list of possible malfunctions out of his mind. He was already trained for any emergency procedure.

"Pax is entering Martian atmosphere," Cassi said. Her deep voice sounded lovely through his suit radio.

As he sat next to Morgan, with Randy and Aiden in back, Diego searched the sky. He turned to the other rover. In the front passenger seat, Vlad shrugged. Behind him, Michelle pointed to a dot of light high in the pink-orange air to the north.

"We see you, Pax." Diego watched the light arc across the sky as he grabbed the wheel and tried to stand in his bulky suit. He spoke no more than necessary. During the landing, their radios sent every word they said in a constant stream to Mission Control. He was talking to the world, but he wanted this to be a private time. Soon he would be able to hold his love again, to enjoy the scent of her braids and the touch of her soft skin.

The dot became a lightbulb and then a flaming object streaking down through the heavens as if slung from a space catapult. He knew Pax would protect her amid the flames, but the sight of her spaceship on fire knotted his stomach.

"Touching down on the intercrater plains two kilometers northwest of Rockhouse," Cassi said, casually naming their surface habitat. "Stay back," she added.

Diego started his rover's motor. His heart raced with it, a rhythm Mission Control would analyze later in data from his suit monitors. With parachutes trailing from its nose, Pax turned upright and fired its retrorockets in bursts, descending too fast. Cassi always liked faster stops than he did.

At last Pax slowed to a few feet per second, like a lunar lander. Billowing dust marked the spacecraft's landing site, so he couldn't tell if it had reached the surface safely. Head pounding hard with his heart, Diego took off in the rover and drove at top speed into the huge dust cloud. "Cassi, we're coming."

"We're right behind him," Vlad said from the other rover.

Turning slightly to Morgan, Diego noticed that the rough terrain caused her to bounce against her seat. "*Lo siento.*" He eased back on the fuel pedal. "Can you see the ship?"

She wiped the dust from her faceplate and pointed straight ahead.

"The landing was successful, with no apparent damage," Cassi reported. "Hello, Ground Commander Diego and rover crews. I'm ready to go through the checklist before exiting."

When he neared Pax, Diego glanced at Morgan and restrained himself from flooring the brake. Before anyone else got out, he jumped to the ground and ran in flying steps toward the air lock. He could barely see the metal hull through the dust. "Pax, your pilot is coming in to help with the checklist."

"Thanks," Cassi replied. "Finally, I get some help around here."

Diego laughed. He no longer cared that their transmission would be played and replayed on every Earth news channel for days. When he finished the checklist with her, though, he would insist that they take a break and turn off the radios. Vlad could find the parts they needed for the landers, and the rest of the crew could load the rovers, while Diego helped his commander readjust to gravity.

∽∾∽∾

Two hours after the landing, Vlad was loading the last water tank onto a big sled when Diego and Cassandra finally emerged from Pax in their spacesuits. She leaned on him as they made their way to his rover. Vlad planned to use the empty tanks from Pax to make a radiation shield at the habitat for Morgan, but he needed to get Jamese's agreement to add this task to the schedule.

Behind Diego's rover, Jamese and Randy were tying down a load of parts and supplies on a smaller sled. "There you are," Jamese said as Diego helped Cassandra into the passenger seat. "We could have used your help."

"Cassandra is off duty for the rest of the day, to adjust to the gravity," Randy said.

"We didn't take the first day off," Jamese said. "Who is going to make up for our lost time here?"

Vlad would get her to agree with constructing the shields by volunteering. This robot woman, who only wanted to stay on schedule, had no right to call people to task. All of them were explorers with important work to do, but they still had human needs and desires.

"I will help make up for lost time," he said. "Taking the water tanks was my idea."

Diego bounded over to Vlad. "What are you doing, *amigo*?"

"If we use these tanks for extra shielding around the habitat, we won't have to dig a hole."

"For Morgan?" Diego held the tank while Vlad tied it down.

"Yes," Vlad said.

"Of course, for Morgan," Jamese said. "Another day of experiments gone for her."

Jamese was so pretty, with those large, pouty lips that she always painted bright red. If only she wouldn't spoil everything with her tongue, Vlad could enjoy spending time with her. At least they weren't transmitting to Earth any more.

"Stop it." Randy said.

"She's right," Morgan said. "I am responsible for taking up a lot of time scheduled for other tasks."

Vlad was glad he had insisted that Morgan rest in his rover while they prepared to return to Rockhouse. She had done more than her share of loading supplies. He knew by the way Randy looked at her that they would get back together. Until they did, Vlad didn't mind protecting her like a big brother. He would get Jamese to agree to the shield somehow.

"What tasks can we all do to make time to build a safety shield?" he asked.

"I can do Jamese's housekeeping chores," Morgan said. "So she'll have more time for experiments."

"You should not do extra work," he said. He hadn't meant to make life more difficult for her. "Who else?"

"I will do my share of the extra tasks," Morgan insisted.

"I'll help in my free time," Aiden said. He crawled out from under Vlad's sled and gave a thumbs up.

"I will, too," Michelle added, waving her good arm. "We could attach the lab to the habitat to save time going in and out of the second air lock."

"Moving the lab isn't in our schedule," Jamese said.

"Just change the schedule, stop squabbling, and take me home," Cassandra said. "Then start building that shield around us."

"Yes, ma'am," Vlad answered his new ground commander. He started his rover.

"I don't think Mission Control will approve this extra work," Jamese said.

Why did she have to make things more difficult than they already were?

Diego vaulted into the other Rover, grinning as he relinquished command to Cassandra. Vlad liked Diego, who also preferred to do things rather than worry about how other people were doing them.

As Vlad drove back across the rocky plains, dodging boulders, he imagined that his visor was colored cellophane through which he saw a red-orange sky that was really blue. The first Viking lander picture, released to the public in 1976, showed a blue Martian sky by mistake. He feared he might not ever see the sky on Earth again in person. He might never watch another sunset with Revka. His eyes watered as the sun climbed higher above the eastern horizon of Gusev Crater. The rover's shadow stretched out to Vlad's right. To take his mind off home, he started planning the radiation shield he would build for the habitat.

ↁↂↁ

That evening all eight of them sat around the wardroom table after dinner to redo their work schedules. Mission Control had sent a revised master schedule for them to modify and agree with. Morgan anxiously searched it in her electronic notebook to see which of her tasks had been reassigned. Her heart sank. All of her sample collections were assigned to Jamese and Randy. They would go out together day after day to do what Morgan had dreamed of for years, while she was stuck in the habitat. She had to find a way to do her full share of work.

"The modifications to the habitat aren't on the schedule," Jamese said with a frown. "How long will they take?"

"If everyone helps, we can get it done tomorrow," Vlad said, smiling.

"I need to start my experiments tomorrow," Jamese said. "I should have started them today."

"The less extra radiation Morgan gets, the more likely the baby is to develop normally," Randy said.

"Maybe she should stay in Pax," Jamese said. "It already has extra shielding."

"By herself?" Cass asked, making eye contact with Morgan and shaking her head almost imperceptibly.

Morgan looked at each face in turn around the table. Michelle and Aiden, who also had experiments behind schedule, appeared to be considering the idea. A stab of fear shot through her at the thought of being alone on a planet so far away from Earth, but maybe it was the best solution. At least she wouldn't be in anyone's way there.

"I'll leave in the morning," she said. "After I rig up a computer link to the lab cameras and equipment to do the analysis work remotely." She hoped they wouldn't agree with her.

"No," Randy said, looking straight into her eyes for a change. "If you needed medical attention, we would be too far away, and we cannot leave one of the rovers parked there. Also, all eight of us living here, the maximum occupancy for this habitat, will provide valuable psychological data for future missions."

"Mission Control approved my return to active duty," she said, looking away.

"Mostly inside, to avoid radiation," Jamese said. "We can move some lab equipment in for you, but we still have to collect your samples, so we have to factor in time for that."

"I could go out and collect my samples when the sun's radiation is low," Morgan said.

"That might work," Aiden said, rubbing his beard.

"We can't schedule like this," Jamese said. "If the radiation is low, you could go out sometimes, but we need a solid plan for getting our work done."

"I can do two hours of extra work a day to make up time in your schedule," Diego said.

"Whoa, there," Cass said, throwing her palms up like stop signs. "We're supposed to be working together on this schedule. Let's consider everyone's ideas."

"Yes," Vlad said. "Let's start with tomorrow. Who will help me refill the water tanks from the power-plant supply and hook them up around the habitat?"

Everyone raised a hand except Jamese and Michelle.

"I can help move some lab equipment inside," Michelle said. She rubbed her sprained arm, still in a sling, and looked at Jamese.

"Oh, all right," Jamese said. "If you're moving the lab, I can't run experiments in it. I'll help with that, too, so we can get the lab attached to the air lock tomorrow."

"Now we're making progress." Cass flashed a smile at everyone. "Morgan, we need you to stay inside and set up your equipment and computer links to the lab."

Morgan looked down at her hands and nodded agreement. Was there no way to even this up, so she would be doing her part as a full member of the crew? Desperate not to be a burden, she blurted out, "If I have to stay in, all of you can leave your cleanup chores for me in return for splitting up my tasks."

Approving grins and nods of agreement met her suggestion around the table. No one liked to take time away from their work for daily household chores in the habitat. Now she would be their drudge.

"The exercise will be good for you," Randy said.

She would rather exercise on the surface. First pregnant woman on Mars, and she gets to do the dishes and laundry and clean the bathroom.

Cass patted her hand. "I'll try to get some excursion time approved for you when the radiation is low. I can go with you in my free time."

Aiden and Vlad immediately volunteered to take Morgan out during their time off.

Jamese did some calculations in her notebook. "If we split up the tasks that Morgan can't do and she picks up our housekeeping chores, we can complete all of our scheduled tasks by working an extra hour a day until the backup ship arrives in fifty-eight days. Then, if we wait two extra days to leave, we'll have time to complete the experiments that should have started running yesterday."

"Let's have a vote on this," Cass said. "All in favor?"

With a heavy knot in her chest, Morgan raised her hand with the others to approve Jamese's new schedule.

"That's it, then," Cass said, holding onto the table to stand up. "Jamese, you can work out the details of our revised plan and submit it to Mission Control for approval. I'm going to see if these rubbery legs can take me to my room."

Diego pranced after Cass through the doorway. Michelle followed, with a friendly nod to the rest. Then Randy left, without looking at Morgan.

"I can show you the design for the shielding," Vlad said to Aiden. "It's in my room." They didn't even glance at her on their way out the door.

Jamese waved at the after-dinner litter in the wardroom. "Thanks for volunteering to clean up." She smiled too sweetly as she left.

Exhausted, Morgan began putting trash into the recycler. She wondered how many hours a day she had just volunteered for.

℃⋙℃⋙

Banging and clanking noises filled the habitat all morning while the men and Cass attached the water tanks around the outside. Morgan finished cleaning up from breakfast just as Michelle and Jamese began depositing her lab equipment on the wardroom table. Morgan was determined to remain calm and friendly to Jamese, no matter what happened.

"You'll probably have to set this stuff up in your room," Jamese said. "We're already cramped in here at meal times."

"I was planning to," Morgan said, making herself smile as she picked up her analyzer.

"Maybe you can find some space in the exercise room," Michelle said, setting down a microscope.

"Then only one person at a time could suit up for going outside," Jamese said.

"Thanks for the suggestion, Michelle, but I have enough room," Morgan said.

Unpacking a container, Jamese spread out the contents to cover the rest of the table.

"It would be easier to unpack the containers in my room," Morgan said.

"I'm just trying to help," Jamese said. "If you don't need help, we should not be wasting our time here."

Morgan's cheeks went hot, so she picked up the analyzer and left, her angry reply unspoken. She would come back later with her sleep net to carry the other instruments.

ოჳიჳ

When she finished installing the lab equipment in her room, Morgan had barely enough space to walk to her bed. She put her hand on her abdomen and moved her palm out to where the baby would grow in two months. She would have just enough clearance to squeeze through.

Someone knocked on the door, and she opened it. Randy stood smiling down at her, like a doctor welcoming his patient. She wished he would drop the professional mask. Why was he here?

"Are you coming to lunch?" he asked.

"I'll be right there, as soon as I finish the setup. Sorry there's no room to invite you in."

He looked disappointed. His distant behavior must be a front, then. He coughed into his fist. "I can walk with you."

She could be professional, too. "It's not far, but okay, if you'd like to."

"You need regular meals to maintain the health of the fetus."

Stepping out into the corridor and closing the door, she looked up at him. "Don't worry, Randy. I love to eat, and I would never let my baby go hungry."

His face turned the color of garnet. "Okay, I will see you in the wardroom," he said, walking quickly away from her.

She went to lunch alone.

CHAPTER 10

Koll followed an aide into Senator Handry's office a few minutes before the Congressional hearing. Thanks to Handry, Koll might be able to get the Senate Subcommittee on Science, Technology, and Space to approve his proposal for the first colony on Mars. Morgan's easy pregnancy had calmed public fears about emigration to another planet, so the lawmakers were willing to consider it.

Maybe, just maybe, Koll would get a colony established on Mars before war destroyed Earth, if he could speed up the timeline and get financing for his trip. Terrorist attacks already plagued the lunar colonies, so they were unlikely to survive. Morgan would be furious with him for hiding her pregnancy at launch time, but eventually she would understand. He would dedicate the Martian colony to the grandparents she lost in the San Francisco attack.

"Welcome, Koll." Senator Handry offered his hand across a huge, teak desk. The aide left and closed the office door. "Is everything ready for the hearing?"

"Yes," Koll said, shaking the senator's hand. "I think my plan could save taxpayers money by starting permanent colonization now rather than using our resources for short visits."

Handry twirled a globe of Mars on his desktop. "What about all the exploration we planned?"

"That can continue, but we don't have to bring everybody back each time." Koll reminded himself to stick to the executive summary. "People who live on Mars can explore it. We can keep sending people there, not only explorers, but also a support staff for them, and families."

"Yes, like we discussed on the phone. Let's go tell the subcommittee about your plan. Even I might get to Mars eventually." As they left the office, the senator's laughter filled the hall.

Joining in to be polite, Koll heard nervousness in his own laugh. Everyone wanted to go to Mars.

They walked silently the rest of the way to the hearing room and then filed in with other attendees. Senator Handry walked over to sit with two other subcommittee members behind a long, mahogany table. Assistants stood in back of the three senators and juggled stacks of papers. Around the room, people spoke softly on cell phones, typed in notebooks, and moved pictures and text around on the tabletop computer.

Handry, the subcommittee chairman, lowered his gavel to begin the session. "Dr. Koll Eriksen, NASA's chief medical officer and ground surgeon for the Pax mission, has a proposal for us."

Koll rose to present his plan while the assistants handed out printed copies. An electronic copy appeared in front of each person seated at the table and on notebooks and laptops around the room. "Mr. Chairman and members of the subcommittee, thank you for the opportunity to appear before you today to present a viable plan for Mars colonization in the near future—"

"Dr. Eriksen," Senator Ella Ramirez said. "You are the most persistent advocate for space exploration I have ever encountered. We've read your plan several times for numerous hearings."

This brought general laughter. Good. It sounded friendly.

"We still don't know if Ms. Zeller can live on Mars without damage to the fetus," Ramirez said. "I think we should wait until the baby is born."

"The data shows a normal pregnancy so far," Koll said. His hopes for easy approval deflated like a balloon leaking air.

"What about radiation?" Senator Neeraj Ragishi asked.

"The Pax crew built an extra shield of water tanks around the habitat," Koll said. There were too many questions for a done deal. He needed to use more words from the questions in his answers. "Also, as you know, NASA is working on a new spacesuit with better protection against radiation."

"We have funding available now," Handry said. "If we wait, the funding could go elsewhere, and we wouldn't be able to establish a colony."

Grateful for Handry's support, Koll smiled at the senators and made eye contact with each one.

The subcommittee voted to send Koll's plan to the Committee on Commerce, Science and Transportation. With Handry's sponsorship, the committee would probably approve the plan. Koll thanked the senators, left the meeting, and climbed into a waiting limo to go to the airport.

If only it hadn't been necessary to deceive a good friend to get the colony started, Koll would feel much better about his actions.

Establishing a place for humans beyond the reach of a nuclear holocaust would be worth it, though, and Morgan would be rewarded for her achievements.

As he rode past the Washington Monument, he imagined a spaceship monument the country would build for Morgan someday. Then he started planning the next phase of his scheme to get to Mars.

CHAPTER 11

A week after Mission Control returned Morgan to active duty, she checked predictions of solar particle events. The levels of solar activity had finally fallen enough for her to go out and collect her own samples. She hurried through her daily cleanup duties. Jamese and Randy had brought back plenty of rocks and soil to keep her busy every afternoon in the minilab in her room, but Morgan couldn't get the flash she'd seen from the lander out of her mind.

Something metal must be out there. What else could cause a reflection like that? At first she had thought it was the old Spirit Rover from the 2004 robotic mission, but the flash was in the wrong place. Anyway, Cass and Diego had visited Spirit two days ago in the hills behind West Spur.

The flash had been on Chawla Hill, just close enough for a four-hour outing. With the protection of her spacesuit, the low radiation wouldn't endanger her baby.

She went to the exercise room where Vlad and Aiden were putting on their suits in the air lock. "Are you sure you have time to go with me today?" she asked.

"Yes, of course," Vlad said. "We're not going to let you go alone. I'll start the rover." He donned his helmet, and Aiden helped him go through the safety checks. Morgan used the computer screen on the wall to find the latest update on solar activity. Still safe.

Vlad exited to go to the outer air lock on the other side of the lab so Morgan would have enough room to put on her suit. She already wore a larger upper torso piece. Aiden helped her with the helmet, and they went through their safety checks together. Then she followed him through the door and the lab. She normally avoided the lab because it wasn't shielded from radiation as well as the habitat. Lucky to go outside at all, she passed through the outer air lock and then climbed into the passenger seat of the waiting rover. Vlad was at the wheel of the open vehicle. Aiden sat in back.

"Where to?" Vlad asked.

"Chawla Hill. I saw a flash there during my descent."

Pulling away from Rockhouse, Vlad said, "You've been keeping secrets from us."

"No," she said. "It's probably nothing, but I'd like to go look."

"Shouldn't we also collect some of the samples that are on the schedule?" Aiden asked. "I mean, in case Jamese and Randy can't get all of them."

The Columbia Hills rolled by on Morgan's right as they traveled toward the last hill. To their left, ruddy plains invited her to explore among centuries-old craters and boulders.

"Are your radios transmitting to anyone else?" Morgan asked.

"We set them for just the three of us," Vlad said.

"Good." She suppressed a grin. "Then I can tell you what I think of Jamese's schedule."

"Better not," Aiden said. "We're not as good at keeping secrets as you. Tell me more about what you saw."

"Probably metal. I thought it was Cardinal at first, but the reflection from Cardinal's hull was bigger."

Vlad turned to wink at her. "So we're going to look for some metal that humans didn't put on Mars."

"Ouch," she said when the rover ran over a large rock. "Please watch the road."

"Yes, ma'am." As they drove around West Spur and past Husband Hill, Vlad whistled the lunar anthem, probably because he knew she disliked the tune.

She didn't mind his teasing because she was finally exploring the surface of Mars. Her dream had come true after all. She had worked so hard for this for so many years. Now she was here, with the small sun high in an ocher sky as they rode past the sienna sand and dusty gray rocks. Nothing could spoil these moments for her. Soon they passed Clark Hill and arrived at the base of Chawla.

She scrambled out of the rover in her thick suit faster than the men. "Let's go."

"We have to follow procedures first," Vlad said as he retrieved a portable habitat. "You know that."

"We're not going to need the tent," she said, partway up the first mound. "Setting that up would cut into our exploration time."

"You sound like Jamese," Aiden said, which brought Morgan up short. Guilt settled into her chest like sediment as she turned and went back down to help them.

"What if you fainted again?" Vlad asked. "We would have only a few moments to get your helmet off, with no time to return to the rover. When you rescued us, we had to bring you into Cardinal fast."

"Oh," she said. "I don't remember."

"Because you were out cold," Aiden said.

"Sorry." These guys didn't have to spend their free time driving her around.

Aiden got the still camera out of the rover.

"Now we can go," Vlad said. "I turned off the rover video. We have to set our suits to broadcast to everyone."

Morgan took the lead. As she walked, she turned on her helmet camera and radio. They climbed slowly. She started describing the terrain in layman terms for the billions of ears that would be listening minutes later, when their video and audio signals reached Earth.

"We're walking through the peaks and valleys of the steep hills, among rocky outcrops. I want to find the place where I saw a big flash of light when I descended in Sparrow, the emergency lander."

"Should we take some samples here?" Aiden asked.

"Yes, we could drill there." She pointed to part of an outcrop and then scooped up some soil next to it. "I'm sure I saw the reflection somewhere around this area."

Vlad inflated the habitat while Morgan and Aiden took samples.

She led them up the hill, stopping to take more samples several times. They went across a small ridge and then down through a little valley. In the sky, the sun sat close to the edge of the ridge, like a flying saucer about to land.

"We have to go back soon," Vlad said.

"I know. I hoped we could find the source of the reflection today."

"We can come back," Aiden said.

"Okay. I guess we should pack up and start down the hill," she said, disappointed. What if it weren't safe to go out again before they had to return to Earth? Were these few hours the only time she would ever get to explore the whole planet?

Well, at least she got that. Sighing, she turned to go. Sunlight glinted off the side of the slope to her right.

"There." She pointed like a hunting dog at the spot where the light had gleamed.

Vlad bounded up the hillside. "I'll fetch it."

"Wait," she said. "We have to document its location and environment before we move it."

Aiden hung back to climb up with Morgan. "Don't over-do it," he said.

"I'm not tired at all." Most of the people on Earth would probably hang on every word, concerned about the pregnant woman climbing hills on Mars. She let him hold onto her arm to make sure she kept her balance. Even with six wheels, Spirit had slipped on the low elevations nearby. One fall might injure the baby and would end Morgan's explorations for the rest of the mission. She could barely restrain herself from running uphill after Vlad. What was it that reflected the light? Just a shiny boulder?

"I don't see anything except rocks," Vlad said. He turned slowly around in a full circle.

"Over to the left a bit," Morgan said as she caught up to him, Aiden right behind her. She moved between two boulders, and then she found it. "Here."

They stared at manufactured metal the size of a door, not rusted, resting in the long shadow of the larger boulder.

"We are not alone," Morgan said before she could think of anything else. Her cliché would replay around the world as words from the astrogeologist when she found the first alien artifact encountered by human civilization. The baby fluttered inside her.

Aiden, speechless for once, took still pictures from all angles. He motioned for Morgan to stand by the metal.

"What is it?" Vlad asked.

Grateful for the nudge, she said to the news audience, "I see a rectangular piece of metal about one meter by two meters, with a polished surface. It's no thicker than paper." Moving next to the long side, she swung her head very slowly from end to end to give viewers a good look at the entire artifact.

Aiden took soil samples near the object while the shadows around them lengthened and the sunlight dimmed. They had to hurry. She reached down and lifted the metal into the air, while Aiden and Vlad kept their helmets steady to record from two different angles.

"The force of gravity here," Morgan continued, hefting the metal, "about one-third the gravity you feel on Earth, doesn't bend this thin sheet of metal. Maybe it's an advanced alloy." She unfastened an electronic marker from her belt and stuck it in the soil. "This area might contain additional artifacts, but we have to return to Rockhouse now. We don't want to be out in the cold after sundown."

"I'll go strike the habitat," Vlad said.

Aiden carried the metal downhill. Morgan followed at a good picture distance, trying to keep her helmet steady to show people on Earth their retrieval of an object manufactured on a different planet. She kept filming until he deposited the metal carefully in the back of the rover. Then she turned her video off and reset her radio for private, three-way conversation.

Exhausted, she pulled herself up into her seat, stunned by their discovery. What did it mean? She had assumed that the metal was of alien origin, but could there be another explanation? Was it manufactured here on Mars, or did it come from other explorers like themselves, from outside the solar system? Maybe it had fallen from one of Earth's failed robot missions, but she didn't think so. She searched her memories for anything from Earth that could have accounted for the object but came up blank.

"Buckle up," Vlad said as he arrived. He stowed the portable habitat in back.

"Oh, I forgot," she said, fastening her belt.

Vlad jumped in and grabbed the steering wheel. The rover bucked when it took off, too fast. She turned to check the artifact. The sun touched the horizon to the west, and its salmon-pink rays lit the strange metal behind them. Vlad repositioned the vehicle to head toward Rockhouse.

Shadows stretched past boulders that blocked the dim sunlight. After sunset, a bluish glow lingered on the western crater rim in the wake of the star. Earth rose to the middle of the glow before they pulled up to the lab air lock. She stared at the pale blue dot, wondering how its billions of inhabitants were reacting to the news of aliens on Mars.

⌀⌀⌀

Morgan imagined she felt the chill of the Martian twilight through her spacesuit as they started to unload the rover in a dark-orange glow. She reached for the metal sample, hoping its significance would thaw Jamese's attitude and bring them all together as a team.

"Go in," Vlad said. "We'll bring your discovery."

"Thanks," Morgan said. "The discovery is all of ours, though. I couldn't have found it without you."

She walked through the air lock, barely feeling her feet. Randy and Jamese waited in the lab, her hand resting casually on his arm.

While Morgan took off her helmet, Jamese glared at her and asked, "How could you exclude the rest of us from something so important?"

"Easy," Randy said. "She needs to lie down after her long excursion."

Caught off guard by Jamese's question, Morgan said, "What do you mean, exclude you?" She went toward the entrance to Rockhouse, carrying her helmet, as she spoke.

"You know what I mean. If you saw something unusual on your descent, you should have asked us to put it on the schedule instead of keeping it to yourself until today."

Morgan decided to postpone the discussion. She really did need to rest. "It was reported during my descent. Can we talk about this after dinner?"

"Yes," Randy said before Jamese could respond. He brushed her hand away. "Or tomorrow."

Vlad and Aiden came in with the metal. Morgan walked back to them as they set it down and took off their helmets. They hugged her, whooping and laughing. Cass, Diego, and Michelle came in through the inside door. All eight of them filled the lab. They stared at the strange object resting on the plastic floor against a table.

"*Madre mía*," Diego said.

"Way to go, Morgan," Cass said.

"Yes, congratulations," Randy added.

"This discovery belongs to all of us," Jamese said.

"Of course it does." Morgan forced herself to smile at Jamese. "We'll list our names alphabetically."

"Backwards, starting with Z," Vlad said.

Aiden nodded so hard his curls covered his face.

"Great find," Michelle said to Morgan. "We have your dinner ready."

"No cleanup for you tonight, either." Randy turned his back on Jamese and took Morgan's arm. "I'll help you out of your spacesuit."

"Thanks," Morgan said. "But someone needs to catalog the artifact." She pivoted to face Jamese. "Would you like to do that?"

Jamese nodded and almost smiled, but her eyes still glared.

Morgan followed Randy to the exercise room. She didn't know how to improve her uncomfortable interactions with Jamese. Why was the engineer always at odds with her? She decided not to think about it anymore. Nothing could spoil her exhilaration over their find. The flash of light she had seen on her descent to Mars had become the most important discovery in history. The honor of playing a part in it thrilled her.

CHAPTER 12

It's an unknown alloy," Morgan said, describing the results of her preliminary tests on the metal piece at dinner the next evening. "I can fold it in half, but it returns to its original shape no matter how I bend it."

"Could you determine whether it was made on this planet?" Vlad asked.

"No. I have to go back to that spot and look for more artifacts." She hoped no one would object.

"Randy and I plan to do that tomorrow," Jamese said. She held up a revised schedule on her electronic notepad.

"I can go." Morgan didn't like the way Jamese said "Randy and I" as if they were a couple. "The sun activity is still low, with no SPEs forecast." The other woman had been monopolizing Randy, and now she was trying to take over the most important work of Morgan's life.

"All of us will go and help," Vlad said. He held his palms up like stop signs, as if he expected no more discussion.

"The rest of you have scheduled tasks that won't get done if you come with us," Jamese said. She set the notepad in the middle of the table and put her hand on top of Randy's. "We can do a thorough search."

"Maybe we should check with Mission Control." Randy looked down at their hands but didn't withdraw his.

Then Vlad spoke the words that Morgan had suppressed for so long. "I don't care about your schedule, Jamese." He stood and spread his long arms wide. "This is the most important discovery in the history of our civilization, and you want to control it." He threw his hands up over his head. "I'm going tomorrow, and so is Morgan." He strode out of the wardroom, the low gravity giving a slight bounce to each step.

"We'll all go," Cass said. "I'll get approval from Mission Control. Jamese, send me your schedule so I can revise it."

"It's my responsibility to maintain the schedule." Jamese looked at Cass with surprise and then glanced up at Randy. He removed his hand from under hers, stood, and picked up his dishes. A stunned expression crossed her face, but she quickly regained a professional demeanor.

Relieved that Randy wasn't backing Jamese up, Morgan started stacking the other dishes.

Cass rose from her seat and flexed her hands at her sides. Anger hardened her eyes into a glare directed at Jamese. "Everything here is my responsibility, which I can delegate to you if I so choose. I'm in charge of the schedule now."

Diego, Aiden, and Michelle slid around the table, one by one, to stand with Cass.

"Good decision," Randy said. He helped Morgan clear the rest of the table.

Jamese turned away and left silently, taking giant strides out the door.

"Thanks." Morgan said to her remaining crewmates. She wondered how Jamese would retaliate.

℘℘℘

The next day all eight of them ate breakfast early and left at dawn in the rovers. On the way, Morgan verified the low solar activity. After they arrived at Chawla Hill, she helped unload cameras, equipment, and supplies onto a sled. Aiden and Vlad started pulling it up the hill.

"Would everyone please set your suit radios and cameras for broadcast to Earth?" Jamese asked. Then she held up the big video camera and started acting like the group's spokesperson for the excursion.

"We're beginning our search for additional alien artifacts," she said for the international audience. "After finding manufactured metal two days ago that didn't come from Earth, we redirected all of our resources into this most important discovery in the history of our civilization."

Although annoyed at Jamese's power grab, Morgan was also relieved that she didn't have to perform the running commentary. She could conserve her energy for the critical work of searching for more objects. Her mind was free to think as they passed over the same rises and troughs as they traversed yesterday. Their suit cameras recorded every step.

Wherever the strange metal came from, they needed more information. They didn't know whether the piece represented an opportunity to make new friends, a threat to humans from advanced aliens, or a window into Martian history. The future of the human race could depend on what they found today. The baby's movement inside her womb as she hiked through the gentle Martian hills filled her with joy. She was grateful for the opportunity to participate in this exploration.

At the boulders where Morgan had found the metal, she interrupted the travelogue. "Excuse me, Jamese. We need to start our search here."

Jamese stopped talking and turned her back on Morgan.

"This is where we found the artifact," Morgan continued. "We need to run the GPR sled, ground penetrating radar—" she added for those listening on Earth. "—over this area first. Then, if you find anything, please remember to take still pictures and catalog its location before you move it."

Cass and Diego set up the plastic habitat while the scientists began the search. Randy and Vlad marked the circumference of the search area. Following Morgan's lead, Michelle and Aiden moved their heads slowly to record every inch of ground.

After training the big camera on them, Jamese resumed her performance. "We're searching the area where we discovered the metal piece. So far, all we see are rocks around here."

As Jamese droned on, Morgan snapped several still pictures of a lumpy area through her helmet camera and entered location data into her sleeve computer. She picked up a rock and dusted it off with a soft brush. Underneath the red-orange coating, the rock was blue, not gray, and it looked symmetrical, with three small holes on two of its opposing sides. "I found something."

Everyone rushed over to Morgan, led by Jamese, who continued her commentary. "We have discovered another possible artifact. It looks dark blue, somewhat rectangular, and small enough to fit in a gloved hand."

Morgan added, "The object has three openings at the same place on opposite sides." She took measurements with the tools on her belt and entered the data into her computer.

"What's this?" Vlad asked from behind her. She turned around as he pulled a square piece of metal, much smaller than her first find, out of the ground.

Next to him, Randy held up a rock. "I think this is like the one that Morgan found."

"Okay, let's proceed slowly," Morgan said. "We have to take time to gather all the data about each piece before you move it."

"Parts," Diego said, picking up more rocks. "These look like mechanical parts scattered around."

Down in a gully, Cass found more metal and said, "I think it's wreckage. Something must have crashed here."

Jumping down to join Cass, Aiden started the tedious cataloguing. Morgan took still pictures of each artifact before he moved it. Then Aiden took over the pictures so Morgan could collect some objects. After she entered all the data for each piece, she handed it to one of the others to package, label, and load carefully onto the sled.

ↄↄↄↄ

When the sled was full, they turned off all the broadcasting equipment and headed for the portable habitat. Morgan went through the clear plastic air lock first, removed her spacesuit, and made a beeline for the curtained facilities in the corner. After cleaning up, she sat in her gray undergarment on a folding chair, exhilarated by their find and not caring how her round belly looked.

"Was it a spacecraft from another planet?" Diego asked while he pulled up a chair next to her.

"Maybe," Cass said as she joined them.

"We have a lot of testing and analysis to do before we can determine what the objects are," Morgan said.

Jamese sat across from her, beaming with excitement. "We're going to be famous."

"We are fortunate to have an opportunity to make such a major contribution to human knowledge," Randy said.

Morgan laughed and looked up into his emerald eyes. "You sound like a brochure again."

"I'm with Randy," Aiden said, his eyes watering. "I knew coming to Mars was important, but I never thought we would find anything this significant." He pushed his untamed hair out of his face and swiped it with the back of his hand.

"*Si*," Diego said. "This is big."

Cass leaned back and chuckled. "Your heads are getting big. We're just doing our jobs."

"Speaking of jobs," Jamese said. "If we go back to Rock-house now and work into the evening, we can get most of our scheduled tasks done."

Vlad looked at her in disbelief. "You keep working. I'm going to celebrate. I saved something special for us to drink on a really great occasion, and this is it."

Standing near the portable radio on the side of the room, Michelle said, "We're getting a message from Earth." She turned up the volume.

"Pax crew, this is Mission Control. Congratulations on a terrific job." Randy patted Morgan's shoulder as the message continued. "Everyone loves the pictures. We're all celebrating your big discovery here. The whole world is partying. We want you to take the rest of the day off and join in the festivities. After that, all scheduled tasks are canceled, except for experiment maintenance, until we can determine how to proceed. Go ahead and start testing the objects tomorrow. Wish we could be there with you. Earth out."

Everyone except Jamese cheered. Morgan smiled at her, hoping she would join their celebration. Jamese's face remained expressionless as she rose and headed toward the corner curtain.

CHAPTER 13

K oll started rigorous training for the journey to Mars and scheduled his ship to leave as soon as possible. His worst nightmare was another nuclear explosion on Earth before he could establish a self-sustaining colony on Mars. An all-out war could extend to the moon and wipe out the colonies there, ending all hope for human survival.

The discovery of alien artifacts on Mars had spurred renewed interest in Koll's colonization proposal. Investors pledged funds for the first colony ship. Company after company offered resources for Martian settlers. Not only did Congress approve and fund his proposal, they also asked that he be appointed to head up the colony.

To finish the planning, he needed more data on the results of the closed-system experiments on Mars. The successful lunar colonies provided a precedent for setting up closed systems on other planets. His engineers just needed to verify which procedures would work the same and which ones they had to modify for the Martian environment. He needed to be on the colony ship before anyone discovered his deception about Morgan's pregnancy.

A knock interrupted Koll's computer work. He locked the screen and then opened his office door to Timon Brown, who wore a dark blue suit and tie. The visit was official.

"Got a few minutes?" Timon asked.

"Sure. Come in." Koll nodded toward the chair next to his desk as he returned to his seat. "What's up?"

"I've been studying your final plan. It looks viable."

"Thanks." Koll hoped his boss was here just to give his blessing to the plan, not to change it. "You probably have a suggestion."

"Yes, I do." Timon crossed his left leg over his right, clasped his fingers around his knee, and leaned back. It was going to be a big change. "In your colonist selection process, I didn't see any provision for families. Your statement to Congress said that we should send families as support staff for the explorers."

"We can send them later, after the colony is set up." Koll kept his irritation at Timon's interference out of his voice. "Also, families would naturally occur from people living together."

Timon uncrossed his legs, leaned forward, and opened his arms, fingers spread wide. His lips stretched across brilliant white teeth into in a smile. "What if we sent existing families?"

"You mean children?" Koll scratched his head. Why would anyone want to risk children before the colony became self-sufficient?

"Well, mostly I mean married couples, but, yes, maybe a child."

Koll got it. "You mean Morgan's child, after it's born."

"Yes, I'd like her to return to Mars right after the current mission. We need her expertise there, and I don't think she'd be willing to leave her baby behind."

"No, I'm sure she wouldn't. She waited so long to conceive." Koll drummed his fingers on the desk. He had to be extremely careful about what he said now. Morgan could spoil his plans if she discovered and disclosed his deception. She knew the importance of starting the colony soon. Still, he wasn't sure she'd forgive him for lying about her pregnancy, even though it was the only time he had ever lied to her. He had to be on his way to Mars before she found out. "I thought Sandi was scheduled to go next."

"Sandi can still go, but we want the top expert following up on our most important discovery. Morgan made the discovery, so she's the expert now. We want her."

"Okay. Well, I could redesign the plan a bit. It might be too stressful for a growing child at first, though. Who would take care of the baby while Morgan was busy exploring?"

"Your support staff, or maybe her parents, if they want to go. Funding is no longer a problem."

"We'll be ready to launch before Morgan returns." He hoped they would be. Koll had been pushing himself and his team hard to leave that early. His chest hurt with anxiety.

"That's great news." Timon stood and smiled again. "Take as many ships as you need to get the colony going. With the new ion plasma ones, you can stagger their departure. Make it work."

After the door closed behind the director, Koll took deep breaths until his heart rate slowed, which relieved his chest pain. Then he unlocked his computer screen to look for more ways to speed up his departure.

CHAPTER 14

Morgan sat next to Randy in the wardroom, her belly against the table, watching the latest news with the rest of the crew. They'd become as popular as rock stars so fast. She was reluctant to return to Earth, where everyone would know her face.

All of the Pax crew had received offers to come back to Mars as colonists. The current mission had more than three months to go, and her crewmates were planning their next trips. Even Jamese looked happy, apparently resigned to being part of a famous team instead of the star. Morgan would gladly trade her renown for a quiet life in which she could focus on her child and her work.

Cass and Diego's wedding was scheduled for two weeks after Pax landed on Earth. Now they could continue their careers without leaving children behind for months. The commander and pilot had been asked to start the first airline on Mars, a NASA operation to carry people around the planet.

Morgan needed to decide what to do after the baby was born. If she came back to Mars, would Randy? She needed to find out.

"I can loop and dive in the sky here," Diego said. He jumped up, extended his arms like airplane wings, and pretended to fly around the small room.

Vlad laughed. "They are calling me a master engineer in the newscasts." He poured an after-dinner drink for everyone, with apple juice again for Morgan. "Have another round." This time Jamese joined in.

"You're a master at getting my recycling system to work," Michelle said as she hugged Vlad. "With the garden Aiden moved here from Pax, we are finally self-sufficient." She looked at her plastic glass. "Except for this."

Aiden raised his glass. "I'll drink to that."

"You'll drink to anything," Michelle said.

Aiden nodded his curly head. "You're right."

"Are you coming back, Randy?" Morgan asked. She held her breath, waiting for the response, wishing that her plans didn't depend so much on his.

"Maybe," he said.

So there it was. She made her face as smooth as a polished stone and looked down at the table so Randy couldn't read her disappointment. Inside, she crumbled. Randy wasn't going to discuss his plans with her, so they must not have a future together.

"You have a better offer?" Vlad asked.

"No. I had planned to retire after this mission and settle near home, but…" Randy glanced at Morgan.

A slight chill went up her spine. Why did he look at her as if she had something to do with his plans? They didn't want the same life style. He seemed friendly now but had made no effort to resume their relationship. The baby would be enough family for her. Her hope of living with him blew away like sand in a dust storm.

If all went well with the birth, she would return to settle on Mars. Cass and Diego, who were like family, would be here, and Koll would arrive soon with his colonists. Maybe her parents would join her to help with the baby. Her brother and sister could come, too, with their families. Timon had said she could write her own ticket.

ᥱᕿᥱᕿ

Testing and cataloging artifacts kept Morgan busy for long hours during the final weeks on the red planet. No one expected her to do their domestic chores any more. They even did hers so she could have more time to analyze their discoveries.

Vlad moved everything except the treadmill and weight bench from the exercise room to the external lab to make room for Morgan's equipment, which he transferred from her room. He also brought the rest of her instruments in from the lab.

Randy worked beside her every day for as much time as he could spare from his own responsibilities. He said he wanted to be nearby in case she needed medical attention. She wanted more with Randy than just friendship, but apparently he didn't. Being near him all the time made her heart ache to be closer.

Morgan felt the baby move daily now and sometimes guided Randy's hand to her growing abdomen so that he could feel the movement too. He never objected to this but didn't go beyond the interest of a physician. She longed for him to move his hand around her waist so she could put her head on his shoulder.

Cass had redesigned Jamese's schedule so that only critical experiments continued, like Michelle's closed-system procedures. The rest of the crew's time was dedicated to excavating the alien site. Every day a team brought Morgan more objects to measure and analyze. She needed a rover at the habitat, in case of emergency, so the others took turns staying behind, to monitor the experiments at Rockhouse. Mission Control refused to let Morgan go to the site again unless the team needed her there.

☙☙☙

One day, a week before the backup ship was due to arrive in Mars orbit, Aiden made another startling discovery. Morgan first heard about it through her audio feed, while following broadcasts from the exploration team.

"Something alive was in this thing when it went down," Aiden said.

"Are you sure?" Cass asked. "I thought maybe it was a robot, like the spacecraft we used to send here."

"Yes, these are definitely biological remains. Looks like some sort of bones."

Morgan flipped a switch to join the conversation. "Morgan here. Before you move anything, please take a lot of still pictures of where the remains are, with markers to indicate the nearest non-biological wreckage. Also, we need samples of the ground around each piece."

"Will do," Diego said. Morgan reset the switch.

Randy, Michelle, and Vlad rushed into the exercise room, crowding Morgan. "What did they find?" Randy asked.

"We don't know yet," Morgan replied. "Maybe some bones. This is more Aiden's territory."

Jamese started broadcasting her commentary to Earth again. "We just found what are possibly biological remains at the alien site."

"Can we go out there?" Morgan asked. "I should see the material before they move it, not just pictures. They need me at the site."

"Maybe," Randy said, looking at her large abdomen, "but it would be better for you and the baby to stay here."

"Solar activity is extremely low right now, and my suit will prevent any bio-contamination."

"I think we should all go," Vlad said. "This is too big a discovery for Morgan not to be there."

"All right," Randy said to Morgan. "If you agree that this is your last excursion before we return to Earth."

She nodded and set her radio to talk again. "Aiden, we're coming out there. Please don't move anything until we arrive."

"You got it," Aiden said. "Woo-hoo. I'm so excited. I need a break anyway, to calm down."

"We don't need more help here," Jamese said.

Her words quelled Morgan's rising exuberance. Morgan didn't respond. Had Jamese forgotten that she was broadcasting to billions?

"Morgan calls the shots on all excavations," Cass said, repeating a recent directive from Mission Control.

The video stream from Jamese went blank.

ေ၁ေ၁

Michelle drove Morgan, Randy, and Vlad to the site. The others emerged from the portable habitat in their spacesuits just as the new team joined them.

Jamese walked up to Morgan and blocked her progress. "Why did you come? We can do our jobs without you looking over our shoulders."

Morgan stopped and waited, without speaking. Anything she said would give Jamese something to criticize. It would be best to let the others handle her.

"Please move aside" Cass said.

"We didn't say we needed her here," Jamese said, not moving. "She doesn't have to take credit for everything."

Randy stepped between the women. "We should turn on the broadcast now, Jamese. Would you mind narrating again?"

"She shouldn't even be outside," Jamese said before she moved out of the way and started recording.

Morgan set her suit camera and radio for broadcast as she started walking uphill. She held back what she wanted to say to Jamese so that it wouldn't reach Earth.

"The rest of the Pax crew came out to see the remains that the exploration team found this morning," Jamese said for the distant audience. "This discovery might prove to be the most significant of all at the excavation site."

"Over here," Aiden said, motioning for them to hurry.

Morgan had never seen his eyes open so wide beneath his untamed forelock, which his communications cap could not contain. She rushed to his side, put her helmet faceplate against his, and said, "Congratulations on your amazing find."

He jumped up and down like a child who couldn't wait to show his mother a new drawing. His boots kicked up sprays of dust each time he bounced off the red soil.

"Come see it."

Morgan walked over to a shallow pit and looked down. Long, tubular objects lay at the bottom like scattered pipes. Could they be bones?

She knelt and leaned over for a closer look. Near the edge of the pit she saw a tiny spot of green. "Michelle, would you please bring me the tweezers?"

"Here." Michelle handed her the foot-long instrument.

Morgan grasped the green object with her tongs and lifted it up in the pale light of the Martian afternoon. The end of the tongs held a ring.

CHAPTER 15

Two nights later, Randy watched newscasts while resting on his bed. The discovery of alien remains on Mars had sent shock waves through the population of Earth. Some religious leaders questioned the authenticity of the find, calling it heresy. Countries were putting their military organizations on full alert and planning space defense systems. New crop circles appeared in grain fields all over the world.

Next morning, he woke up to several directives from his new Air Force boss. In an emergency session, Congress had voted to place NASA under military control.

When he joined everyone for breakfast, Jamese was saying to Morgan, "Now see what you've done."

Randy did not know how to defuse the situation. Both women were attracted to him, which made his stomach churn. Jamese had never understood that he considered her just a friend, even when they used to go out. She acted like he was holding back because they were on a mission together. He tolerated her intimate touches and held back from Morgan to avoid sending Jamese over the edge. Her behavior was unstable, and they still had to function as a team for another week on Mars and three months of travel back to Earth. Still, he

spent as much time as he could with Morgan, in an odd com-
bination of pleasure and torture that he had never experienced.
If he and Morgan became intimate again, Jamese might find
out and ruin the mission for everyone. She had already noticed
their attraction to each other. He could not hold Morgan or tell
her how he felt until the mission was over.

He hoped Morgan would still want him then. He wanted
to reach out and move his hand across her abdomen, where
their baby grew.

"I've just been doing my job," Morgan was saying to
Jamese from across the table. Randy sat next to different people at meals so Jamese would not react when he sat by Morgan.

"Your job was to complete the planned assignments,"
Jamese said. "Most of them were never done. Now the rest of
our experiments are canceled because of the new directives to
look for more artifacts. We have only a week to repair the
landers."

Vlad waved his hand to stop Jamese's tirade. "Why are
you so upset? Diego and I have the landers almost ready to go.
I don't mind working twice as much this week to help the
world understand these aliens better."

Jamese turned on him, her cheeks reddening to match her
large lips. "You didn't just have the Air Force question your
family and investigate your entire life in detail to get top-secret
clearance." Her black eyes darted from face to face around the
table.

Was she escalating into an anxiety attack now? Randy
would have to intervene somehow.

"It is surprising that your government has not always re-
quired top-secret clearance for their astronauts," Vlad said.
"I've always had it."

"Ours does now," Jamese said with a frown. "Thanks to Morgan."

"Wait a minute," Aiden said, jumping out of his seat. "We should thank Morgan. Without her, we wouldn't be alive, and I wouldn't have found the alien remains. This is the most exciting time of my life."

The others nodded agreement. Some said "Yes" or "Right on." Jamese rolled her eyes.

Morgan looked down at the rest of her food, apparently embarrassed by the praise. Randy wanted to take her away to his room. Instead, he tried to change the subject. "Should we finish eating and get ready to follow those directives?"

"Quit trying to manipulate us," Jamese said. "Being the medical officer doesn't give you the authority to control our conversations."

Jamese had never been openly hostile to him. Her behavior was becoming more erratic.

Morgan cleared her dishes and left the room without speaking. The others followed, one by one, until only Randy and Jamese sat at the table.

"I'm just trying to help," Randy said.

"I don't need your help or your interference."

"What do you need?"

"I need you to quit bothering me." She got up, tossed her breakfast remains into the recycler, and left.

Randy sighed. He would probably have to report her behavior, which could affect her career. Before he did that, though, he wanted to try one last time to be her friend. He could make sure Jamese understood that their relationship was over. Maybe telling her how he really felt about Morgan would work.

෨෧෨

Cass assigned Morgan to run tests, with Randy's help, while everyone else went out in the rovers to pull Cardinal upright. If this effort succeeded, Vlad and Diego would finish the repairs today and start testing the lander, and the others would continue excavations.

Morgan was preparing to examine the alien ring under a microscope when Randy strode into the exercise room.

"Hi," she said, glad to have his company even if he didn't want more than that. She needed to find out for sure whether or not he did.

"What are we doing this morning?" he asked in a professional tone while he pulled on surgical gloves. His muscles bulged under a gray T-shirt.

"Examining this." She held the ring up on a microscope slide, wishing he weren't so detached. "If it was meant for wearing, it came from a thin finger."

The golden circle of metal, tinged with purple, closed against a green gem.

"Hey, it matches your eyes." She instantly regretted the comment.

"Could it be a gem?" he asked.

"I don't think so. It looks artificial to me, but we'll find out." She enjoyed standing near him. Forcing herself to keep her hormones in check, she said, "Would you mind sorting those objects on the table?"

"Not at all." He turned his back and started moving the objects around.

She placed the slide in the holder under her microscope and looked through the eyepiece. "You have to see this."

"What?" He rushed to her side.

"It's some kind of electronic device."

As he leaned over the scope, she resisted an urge to touch him. Warmth spread across her face.

"Incredible." He straightened up and smiled. "Something of beauty with a practical purpose."

Lowering her head to the microscope, she said, "I need to tell Jamese about this."

Vlad's voice came through the wall radio, which patched into the spacesuits of the excursion teams. "We're pulling out now toward Cardinal."

"Good luck," Randy said.

"Jamese," Morgan said. "The green part of the ring looks electronic. I'm going to hold up on testing it until you get back."

"Thanks," Jamese said. "I'll look for electronics at the site." She sounded more like herself than she had at breakfast.

Randy walked back to the objects he'd been sorting. "Which of these do you want next?"

Alone with him for the first time in several days, Morgan had trouble concentrating. She wanted to know if she had a future with him. The baby turned a somersault in her womb.

"Let's start with the smallest one," she said, trying to keep her tone objective.

He carried the object to her in a flat tray. She put it under the microscope. He hovered next to her, as if he weren't sure what to do, so she stood up.

"I should show you how to start one of the tests," she said.

His face broke into another smile. "Whatever you want me to do."

Morgan felt happiness rise in her like the sun moving through the morning mist above Gusev Crater. She wanted Randy to put his strong arms around her. So tired of being alone, she wanted to share everything with him.

"Here." She moved toward a small table with some lab equipment set up near the weight bench. "We need to test the soil that we brushed off the objects for organic material."

Clumsy in her changing, growing body, now nearly six months pregnant, she tripped slightly on a metal strip that anchored the bench to the floor. Randy caught her and held her much longer than was necessary to restore balance.

For a few moments, she enjoyed melting into his embrace. Morgan realized he had been hiding his feelings. Her heart raced.

"Thanks." She stepped back and held onto the bench.

His face reddened. He must not have meant to reveal so much. Knowing that he still cared about her was enough for a while.

She would wait until he was ready to talk about it. In what she hoped was an objective tone, she said, "Let me show you how this experiment goes."

Now she knew what was bothering Jamese. The other woman saw her as a rival not only for professional recognition but also for Randy's affections. He was obviously keeping his distance from Morgan to avoid more tension among the team, doing his job.

She went back to her microscope while he started the experiment. At least she would have his company for the rest of the morning.

The radio interrupted with Jamese's voice, "Randy, are you there?"

"Yes."

"When we get back, will you have time to help me unload and catalog the artifacts?"

"If Cassandra does not have another assignment for me, I will."

Jamese was not going to let Morgan enjoy her time with him.

"I'm sorry you got stuck inside today," Jamese said.

Randy grinned at Morgan before he answered. "I am happy to help wherever I can."

CHAPTER 16

Five days before the backup ship, Pax II, would arrive, Diego and Vlad took fuel from the power plant out to the second lander to perform final testing. The repairs had been simple after they got the parts from Pax. They had fixed Cardinal and finished testing it. Diego hoped no one would need to use the emergency lander. It was their backup because it could carry only two people, three in a pinch, which meant he would have to take four trips into orbit, with three risky landings and refueling each time.

"How long does it take to refuel and run the tests?" Vlad asked from the passenger seat of the rover.

"We can do it in two or three hours," Diego said.

"Good. Your Air Force boss wants me to spend the rest of the day looking for aliens."

"Me, too, and I'm just a pilot."

"A first-rate pilot."

"Thanks."

Cassi's voice broke in over the radio. "Diego, check your weather report. A dust storm is brewing."

"Oh, I thought you were sending me bad news," Diego said. He punched up the report on the rover screen and cursed.

"You're fortunate we're not broadcasting," Vlad said. "How far away is the storm?"

"It's in Hellas Basin," Cassi said. "Looks like it might reach us in a few days, maybe cover the whole planet."

"*No problema*," Diego replied. "Cardinal can take off in anything."

"But we have to load Cardinal and get into it before the worst of the storm hits," she said. "Mission Control has reassigned you two to loading as many of the artifacts and supplies as you can today, after you test the second lander. They don't want everything full of dust."

"We can do that." Diego preferred loading to digging for pieces of a ship that was probably hundreds of years old.

"I have more good news for you," Cassi said. Diego heard reluctance in her voice. "We have to take both landers up to carry all of the alien objects and remains."

"What?" Vlad reacted in surprise. "Your government had us test everything here and take pictures so we wouldn't have to bring it back."

"That changed when the military took over. They want to put every scrap that we found in a secure facility and do their own testing."

Diego didn't want to argue with Cassi, but it would be safer for all of them to be together in Cardinal. "We can fit it all in the big lander if we leave behind the extra water and supplies. Pax II will have those."

"The news gets better," she said. "Because of the growing dust storm, Mission Control wants Cardinal to leave early, with all the artifacts, and wait for Pax II in orbit. So we're going to need all that water and supplies to stay alive until the big ship comes."

"That is insane," Vlad said.

"Better not let the brass hear you say that. They're not budging on this. Make sure you get that little lander in top shape because it's your lifeboat."

"Let me understand this," Diego said. "Mission Control wants you to orbit the planet in a small lander, hoping to survive until Pax II arrives, while Vlad and I wait in a dust storm to take a tiny lander up after the ship gets here?"

"That's the Air Force plan." Cassi sighed. "I tried my best to change their minds, but they want me to pilot Cardinal and you to bring up Sparrow later. They said Vlad needs to stay behind with you to help fix your lander in case something goes wrong again."

Diego was afraid to ask the next question because he already knew the answer. In spite of being honored and celebrated as Earth's heroes for exploring Mars, the Pax team was expendable. "What if no one survives?"

"They can bring Cardinal back to Earth remotely," Cassi said with no emotion in her voice.

Vlad stated what Diego was thinking. "So the alien artifacts are more important to them than our lives."

❧❦❧

The next day, Morgan was packing artifacts in the exercise room when Jamese strode in holding a notepad that flashed yellow light.

"I hope you finished cataloging everything. My database is missing some items,"

"Of course I did." Morgan sighed. Soon they would be in space for three months with nowhere for Jamese to go during the day, no place to get away from her. No matter what Jamese said, Morgan was not going to waste time arguing with her. "I'm uploading the data now."

"Don't snap at me." Jamese set the notepad, still flashing, on the weight bench and stood with her hands on her slim hips. Her full lips pouted as her obsidian eyes scoured Morgan from under even bangs. Her straight, black hair flowed to the middle of her back. "We wouldn't have to rush through this and leave early if you were in a condition to tolerate a dust storm." She looked at Morgan's belly, which had grown rapidly at the end of her second trimester.

The dust storm kept growing as it approached them, so everyone was preparing for an early departure. Whatever they didn't need before they left had to be loaded into the landers as soon as possible. Michelle and Aiden were packing the lab while the rest of the crew drove supplies to Cardinal.

"I'm not snapping, just answering your question." Morgan wondered why Randy would ever choose her, with no waist and dependent on everyone for her survival, over this self-sufficient beauty. Although Jamese's oversized mouth detracted from her delicate, porcelain face, men seemed to prefer thick lips.

"Why don't we just clear the air right now?" Jamese pointed a polish-tipped finger at Morgan. "I've had enough of all this catering to you. Your helpless act is getting boring. It still brings the men running, but I can see through it. You're using your condition to control this mission."

The words brought back Morgan's guilt, about changing the mission plans, and some dizziness. Without breaking eye contact with Jamese, Morgan sat down awkwardly in the chair behind the long table that held unpacked artifacts. Randy was gone for the morning, and no one else could hear them. The baby started kicking inside her.

"If you want to be with Randy, go ahead and pursue him," Morgan said, tired of avoiding the subject. "I don't want to fight about it." If Jamese thought she could still win Randy back after failing for months, let her try. He might not want an instant family, anyway.

"What are you talking about?"

"I know you care for him, and you think I'm in the way."

"Maybe you need some medication. Or is this another manipulation? It's not what I came here to discuss, and your attempt to change the subject won't work." Jamese walked over to the table, leaned in, and put her face close to Morgan's. Her breath smelled like raspberry mint. "Are you going to stop trying to control everything we do?"

"Do what you want." Morgan stood up and resumed packing, determined to remain calm. "I need to get my work done."

"This conversation isn't over until you agree to stop interfering with our plans." Jamese took hold of Morgan's lower arm to prevent her from wrapping items in plastic sheeting. "Look at me."

Red fingernails pressed against Morgan's skin as she tried to shake loose from the grip. No matter what, she wouldn't let herself argue with the other woman. Morgan turned slowly to face her. "Tell me what you would like to hear so I can say it and get back to work."

Releasing Morgan, Jamese pressed her lips together until they looked almost normal. Her notepad beeped. She stuffed it into a leg pocket without checking the screen, grabbed a package of artifacts, and strode out the door. Her angry steps made her bounce slightly in the low gravity, like a silly walk in an old Monty Python show.

ℰↃℰↃ

Morgan had lunch ready and was sitting in the wardroom when Randy returned, followed by the others. She hoped everyone would talk about their tasks and avoid more complex subjects, like the impending rendezvous with Pax II in two separate landers.

"What are your assignments this afternoon?" she asked.

Randy sat next to her while everyone took seats around the table, Jamese on the other side of him.

"I am supposed to move supplies from Pax to the emergency lander," he said.

"With my help," Jamese said. She filled her plate with vegetables from the lab garden.

"Diego and I are going to test Cardinal and top off the fuel, water, and oxygen tanks," Vlad said, "after we load your samples."

"We have to do this every day now," Diego said. "Tomorrow we have to start testing and refilling the emergency lander, too."

"What about the rest of you?" Morgan asked. She had to force herself to eat because her stomach still churned from the morning's confrontation with Jamese. In a few days there would be no more fresh vegetables. They could not make room in Cardinal for the little garden that Aiden had nurtured so carefully and transferred to Rockhouse from Pax. They would be back on ship's rations all the way home.

"We're staying here with you to pack everything we can in Rockhouse," Cass said. "It all gets loaded tomorrow, in case we have to take off earlier than planned."

"The storm is still three days away," Michelle said. "But it could start spreading faster."

"Couldn't we take some of the plants?" Aiden asked.

"You can take some samples and seeds," Cass replied. "But we won't have room for you to maintain plant growth while we wait in orbit for Pax II."

Jamese wore a low-cut red T-shirt that stretched tightly across her small breasts. Morgan hadn't seen her wear the shirt before.

"Please pass the rice," Jamese asked Randy, touching his left arm with the tips of her fingers. She had painted her fingernails the same red as her lipstick and shirt after she left the exercise room this morning. Morgan wondered if her toenails were red, too, and if she had taken in her pants to fit tighter.

Randy not only passed the rice, he also put some on Jamese's plate for her. She blinked her eyelashes rapidly and said, "Thanks."

Amid the hum of conversation around the table, no one else noticed this interchange. Morgan wondered how much of the personal weight allotment Jamese had used for makeup.

"Mmm, this is so good," Cass told Morgan. "All those years fixing dinner for your family was great training for preparing Martian meals."

Everyone ate a lot.

"Yes," Vlad said. "If it weren't the middle of the day, we would have a toast to the chef."

Jamese looked irritated for a moment but kept silent. She smiled up at Randy and offered him half of her cake. He took it.

"Thank you, Morgan," Michelle said, standing and clearing her place.

Most of the others also thanked Morgan. She volunteered to stay behind and clean up, glad they had gotten through a meal without any problems. She tried not to look at Randy and Jamese, who left last. At the door, Jamese looked back over her shoulder and smiled like the Cheshire cat, mouthing "thank you" with her bright red lips.

Morgan tried to smile back, reminding herself that they would be in spacesuits for the rest of the day.

೧ඬ೩

At Pax, Randy tied down the supplies while Jamese went inside to check an experiment. She had been pleasant during the rover ride, even charming as she pointed out particularly colorful boulders and interesting patterns of waves in the sand to share with him. At her suggestion, he had set his suit radio to just two-way transmissions, which she said would be less strenuous for them. She was right.

As he reached under the rover to tie the last knot, his back went out. He couldn't straighten up, but he could walk slowly in a bent position. Pain radiated from his lower back.

He would have to ask Jamese to finish tying the load so they could get back to Rockhouse. He called the Pax radio and said, "Jamese, are you almost ready to leave?"

"Would you mind if I visited my old room for a few minutes?" she asked. "I'll probably never be on Pax again, and I need a break."

"My back is out. We need to finish loading and go."

"I can finish. Come in and rest."

"Okay, but we need to leave in an hour." If he could use the facilities on Pax, he would not have to go in his suit. He hoped he could get the suit off.

He went through the air lock into the exercise room, where Jamese was waiting in her thermal undergarment with ibuprofen, a bag of water, and an ice pack. She set them down, removed his helmet and gloves, and then handed him the medicine and water.

He took the pills. "Thanks."

"You're welcome. Do you want me to put the ice pack on your lower back?"

He nodded and started to take off his spacesuit. She helped him undress to his diaper.

"Where does it hurt the most?" she asked.

He pointed to the sacroiliac joint in his lower right back, and she taped the pack there.

"Would you like me to get a urinal from the medical bay?"

"No, thanks. I can manage."

Bent double and trying not to groan aloud, he hobbled down the corridor and into the tiny bathroom. He could not straighten up enough to close the door, but by moving as little as possible, he managed to relieve himself, refasten the diaper, and clean his hands.

When he emerged, Jamese waited in the black pants and red shirt she had worn at lunch, with bare feet and red toenails.

"I thought you were going to your room," he said.

She flashed her teeth in a beautiful smile. "I did, just to freshen up."

Her clothes fit well, revealing every curve. She had brought them with her, somewhere in her spacesuit, so she must have planned this stopover. It was too bad that he did not feel more than friendship for her because he missed holding that sensuous body. But he loved Morgan now.

The air felt too hot. Jamese must have set the ship's temperature for indoor clothing, which was odd for a brief stay.

"Here," she said, "I brought you a shirt and shorts from the ship supply so you can relax until your back feels better."

"Thanks." He took the clothes and moved slowly toward his old room to change.

"Do you need help?"

"No, thanks," he said without turning around.

He opened the door and eased himself into the room head first, still bending because of the pain. Just in case she decided to help anyway, he locked the door. Then he took off the diaper, unfolded the table from the wall and held onto it with one hand for support as he slowly pulled on the shorts with the other hand, wincing at every movement. He could not get the T-shirt on. Each time he tried to put the shirt over his head, a spasm in his back forced his arm down.

"Come look at this plant," Jamese called from down the hall.

Barefoot and carrying his shirt, he limped to her room. A thriving plant covered the fold-down table.

"How did it last so long?" he asked. Then he noticed light streaming through a viewport that had been covered by the water tanks before they removed them for the radiation shield around Rockhouse. Also, Jamese had rigged up a self-watering and feeding system around the plant. She was a brilliant engineer.

"My last experiment is a success," she said, bouncing off her bed. She rubbed his hurt back softly. "You know I can fix this with a massage, like I used to."

He would be able to walk normally, with less pain, if he let her knead his back, but her massages used to lead to intimate touching. This must be her plan. Still, their return trip in the harsh environment would be more dangerous if he had limited range of motion. He would have to make sure it was just a massage.

Jamese had been so nice lately, pitching in to help whenever she could, that Randy was less worried about her mental state. She had even encouraged him to share his feelings about Morgan. He and Jamese were still good friends, and he thought she had accepted that, but maybe not.

"Lie on your right side," she said.

He climbed onto on her bed, which had a floral scent. As he lay in a fetal position, she kneaded his sore muscles.

"Ahhhh," Randy moaned. All the tension from worrying about everyone's health during the changing mission leaked out of his body. The back pain dulled until he was able to stretch out his legs. The medicine was starting to work, too.

"Roll onto your stomach," she said. When he did, she straddled him. The gentle pressure of her hips on his alarmed him, because he enjoyed it.

She leaned forward to rub his shoulders. He did not want her to stop sitting on him, but he would have to get her off.

"Do you remember when we used to make out?" she asked in his ear, her breasts touching his upper back.

Randy felt a stirring in his groin. Uh-oh. This is definitely what she wants.

He turned over to face her, trying to make eye contact with her sultry pupils. She sat back and started massaging his thighs, making him grow stiff. His body wanted hers so badly that he did not trust himself.

"Stop," he said.

"Stop what?" Her lips pursed into a pout. "I haven't finished the massage."

"We should not be doing this."

"Why not?" She brought her face down to his, their lips a centimeter apart, her nipples resting on his chest. "No one else is here. Who would know?"

"I would. Please stop. I told you that I feel only friendship for you."

"Friends can have a good time," she whispered. She rose to her knees and looked down between them. "You want to." While her hands massaged his lower abdomen, her lips pressed against his. She moved her tongue into his mouth.

Instinctively, he put his arms around her, like he used to back on Earth. He no longer felt any pain, nearly consumed by his urgent need for closeness. He had been alone so long. She stretched her body out on top of his before he broke off the kiss. Morgan was alone, too.

Extracting himself and sitting up, he said, "Jamese, you are beautiful and alluring, but I told you I love Morgan. Your massage really helped my back. Thank you. Could we please remain just friends?"

She stomped out of the room without answering. Randy went to lie down on his bed for a few minutes, angry with himself for allowing the massage to get out of control. He should have been stronger and stopped her right away. Jamese had tempted him, but he really wanted Morgan. Now he was sure that he wanted to marry her, spend the rest of his life with her, wherever she was. Hoping that what had just happened would not interfere with them getting back together at the end of the mission, he put his thermal undergarment back on and went to the exercise room to suit up.

Jamese, already in her spacesuit, was going through the safety checks with Cassandra by radio. She finished and entered the air lock without acknowledging his presence.

He put on his suit and called Cassandra to go through his safety checks. "Why did you remove your suits?" she asked.

"I wanted to use the facilities here and take a break."

"Oh."

Embarrassed that Cassandra knew he and Jamese had been resting together in Pax, he hoped Morgan was not listening to the conversation. He avoided mentioning his back problem because telling about Jamese's massage would be worse.

℘ℑ℘

In her room at Rockhouse, Morgan had heard Cass take Jamese through the suit safety checks and then Randy. A knot of anxiety formed in Morgan's chest. Why were they out of their suits on the ship, where there was room to lie down together? Had Jamese succeeded in her pursuit of Randy? Morgan had been sure he didn't want Jamese, that he was just hiding how he felt to keep peace, but maybe she had misunderstood. Maybe Randy needed comfort, and Jamese was there to provide it while Morgan was restricted to the habitat.

Tears would not come to relieve her aching heart. She felt movement inside herself and placed her hands on her rounded abdomen. Right now all she could worry about was getting safely on the return ship to Earth. Coming down here was not a good idea. She needed to go home and take care of her baby. Randy did not want her. Her cheeks flamed and her hands trembled as she finished packing her room.

൭൭൭

At dinner, Randy came into the wardroom and sat by Morgan. Jamese entered without glancing at him and sat next to Aiden. Morgan wondered why Jamese and Randy were avoiding each other now, after they had been so friendly this morning. At least they weren't acting like a couple. Confused, she relaxed enough to get her food down. Maybe she would get a chance to talk to him tonight. Tired of guessing, she had to find out what he wanted. She and the baby could return to Mars without him, but she needed to know.

"We're all ready to take off," Vlad said.

Jamese looked at Aiden and said, "What are we going to do the next two days?"

"We have to clean up everything here and leave Rockhouse ready for the next team," Cass replied. "When all of that's done, we can rest until takeoff."

Diego nodded. "Also, we need to test the landers and top off the fuel and oxygen tanks again."

"You get to do that," Cass said. "I'm going to stay here, put my feet up, and supervise."

Vlad passed around bags of vodka and apple juice for Morgan.

Jamese took her bag with a smile and raised it for the toast, even though her schedules had been scrapped. She flirted with Aiden the way she used to flirt with Randy, as if the men were interchangeable. Randy did not look at her.

After the meal, everyone seemed to be pairing up to enjoy their last days on Mars. Cass and Diego left hand in hand. Michelle giggled at Vlad on their way out. Aiden offered his arm to Jamese and said, "Good night," with a toss of his curls.

She looked back as if she wanted to make sure Randy saw her leave with Aiden. Randy ignored her and started cleaning up.

"I want to talk to you," she said.

"Yes. We should go talk in my room. Someone might come back here to get water or something."

"All right." She followed him, dreading the conversation, but she wanted to know what was going on.

In Randy's room, they sat at his small table as they had sat at hers the first time he came to her room on Pax. Except here on Mars they didn't have to strap themselves down.

"Randy," she said, starting a conversation she would rather avoid, but determined to find out what kind of relationship they still had. "I think it's time we..." Her words disappeared under his steady gaze.

"Please let me talk first," he said. "It might change what you want to say."

Anxiety tightened her chest. He took her right hand in both of his and leaned forward. Her arm tingled with pleasure.

"I foolishly let myself get into a situation this afternoon that should not have happened," he said, dropping his head.

"You don't have to tell me anything." Her insides churned. She wanted to talk about their future, not about Jamese. "It's none of my business."

"Yes, it is your business if you want it to be. I would rather not tell you because it was insignificant, but you must have found out that I was alone with Jamese inside Pax for a while."

She wished he wouldn't say "alone with Jamese" as if it mattered to him.

"Nothing really happened, but it almost did."

She looked down, pulling back her hand. She didn't want to hear any more. "I think I should go lie down in my room." She forced herself to make eye contact with him and started to get up. "Excuse me."

His eyes glowed like jewels. "Wait, please let me finish before you go."

Was he going to cry? She sat back down.

He ran his hands through his hair. "My back went out while I was loading the lander. Jamese gave me a massage to fix my back, but then she kissed me, and, out of habit, I started to respond."

Morgan turned away. Jamese had touched his bare shoulders and back, running her hands all over his skin, and even put her mouth on his? The image of her sitting astride a half-naked Randy made Morgan dizzy. Or was he naked? She stood up and grabbed the door handle.

"I told Jamese to stop. Nothing else happened because I love you."

Her back to him, Morgan froze with her fingers on the door handle. The words she had longed to hear had just come out of his mouth, but he said them because of Jamese. A heaviness smoldered in her chest. She turned to face him.

"Why have you ignored me, then?" She thought it was because of his job, but she wanted him to say it.

He stood and leaned over the table, so close she could feel his breath on her cheek.

"This borders on violating doctor-patient confidentiality." He sat back down and then stood up.

"Just tell me what you think, Randy, the nonmedical version." Her voice was calm, but angry words waited inside her, like magma in a volcano, threatening to erupt. "Why?"

"Because I thought Jamese still wanted a relationship with me." His face looked bleak now, as if he wasn't convinced by his own explanation. "Part of my job is to help ensure the mental stability of the crew."

"So what happened after your massage was a professional reaction?" Morgan said. Her sarcastic tone sounded ugly. Even though his words made sense, she knew he had not wanted to stop.

He looked at the floor, shook his head, and said in a husky voice, "I was tired of being alone, but then I remembered that you were alone, too."

She wanted to run, to get to her room before she shouted irrational accusations at him. All this time she could have been with him, but he had kept her at a distance because of his responsibilities. He let his guard down only for Jamese. Yet what happened was partly Morgan's fault because she had given Jamese a green light to pursue him. She could let that end everything with him now, or she could at least try to salvage their friendship. He had stopped because he loved her.

As Randy lifted his head, resignation painted his face. "Do you still have something to tell me?"

Walling off her pain to think through later, Morgan reached up to hold his cheeks and said, "I love you, too."

He put strong arms around her and held her tightly. "We have to wait until the mission is over."

"I know," she said, her voice muffled against his chest. Uncertainty still raged inside her. She looked up and asked, "What about returning to Mars?"

"Well," he said, his eyes distant. "My dream has always been to settle in the South, start a private practice, and raise a big family. I want my children to grow up near their relatives."

"Oh." She let go and stepped back. Like molten lava cooling, her hope of a future with him coalesced into a lump within her. Love was just a feeling. It couldn't make two people want the same things. Her plans to settle on Mars would never fit into his dream life.

"But we can talk about the future," he said, reaching for her.

Trying to get away before she lost control, she repeated his words, "We have to wait until the mission is over." Then she left his room and hurried down the corridor toward hers.

"Morgan, please wait," he called after her in a deep, intense voice she had never heard before. Anyone listening would know he was upset.

She kept walking away from him in long steps.

※※※

The next morning at breakfast, Jamese and Aiden arrived together, holding hands. Morgan was relieved to see Jamese with someone other than Randy. Aiden never tried to keep secrets, and Jamese apparently wanted everyone to know.

Randy didn't seem bothered by the new couple as he took the seat next to Morgan. He wasn't giving up then. She needed to figure out whether he really cared about her or thought he should take responsibility for the baby, before she told him that he is the father.

"Did you sleep well?" Jamese asked Randy with a bright smile. She offered him some of her fruit.

"Yes, thank you," Randy said, barely glancing at her.

"Everyone has the day off," Cass said. "We need to rest before taking the landers into space."

Morgan longed to spend the day resting with Randy, but she couldn't do that unless she knew what he wanted.

Diego patted Cass's arm. "You can sleep if you want, *hermosa*. I'll do all the work."

"Stop that." Cass pulled her arm back, and everyone laughed.

"Diego and I have to test the landers and top off the tanks," Vlad said.

"*Si*, we'll have plenty of time to rest when we leave, so why not work now?"

"Okay. You two don't get a whole day off, but you can still relax some. We want everyone bright and bushy tailed in case anything goes wrong."

"My tail is already bushy," Aiden said, shaking his unruly locks.

"I can braid it for you," Jamese said, laughing. She glanced at Randy, who looked at his plate and kept eating his reconstituted eggs.

Aiden rose and grabbed her hand. "Take me to the beauty salon."

As she stood, she asked Morgan sweetly, "Would you mind cleaning up for us?"

"Not at all," Morgan replied, hoping to speed Jamese's departure. She started clearing the table to get the chores out of the way so she could talk to Randy as soon as everyone else left.

"Let's have another toast," Vlad said. "To love." He looked at Michelle, who flushed.

"A toast in the morning, before you go out to test the landers?" Cass asked.

Still looking at Michelle, Vlad added, "I'll be back at lunch with the vodka." He and Diego left, followed by the others.

Morgan wondered if Vlad and Michelle had slept together, too. They wouldn't tell anyone if they had. Morgan felt alone and untouched, single without any prospects. Even a hug would be nice.

Randy finished his meal, got up, and grinned at her. She managed to smile back at him briefly.

"Can we talk?" she asked.

"Yes," he said. "But I have to finish some reports first."

As she watched his strong back disappear through the doorway, Morgan wondered if he was avoiding her again.

CHAPTER 17

The NASA brass was already discussing the Martian dust storm in the conference room when Koll Eriksen arrived. The storm might give Koll another opportunity to speed up the colonization schedule.

"Are we really going to let them take off in the worst dust storm of the century?" Timon asked. "When the storm hits Gusev, the winds can blow more than three hundred miles per hour, with visibility less than four meters."

Koll took a seat near one end of the long conference table. Managers of the Pax mission support team and the Mars program sat facing their new Air Force bosses.

"They'll have no visibility," Colonel Charles Gray said. He and his military aides wore dress uniforms decorated with rows of medals. Their hats rested on the conference table in front of them.

Senior NASA staff members manipulated graphs, statistics, and projections with their hands on the lighted tabletop. Their assistants stood around the walls or sat in small chairs working on laptops.

"We don't need visibility," Jonathan Holt, designer of the emergency lander, said. "They can fly on instruments. We could even fly the landers from here if we had to. The orbital insertion and docking need to be done automatically, anyway."

"What about radio attenuation?" asked Clay Yamoto, the communications officer. "It could interfere with remote commands."

"Then the landers could sit tight until communications improved," Jonathan said.

Koll looked up at the fuzzy red globe on the huge wall screen at the other end of the room. The caption read, *Planetwide dust storm in two days.* Cardinal could leave tomorrow with enough oxygen, fuel, and supplies to support the crew until Pax II arrived, forty-eight hours from now. Takeoff of the emergency lander had to wait for the ship because the tiny vehicle could support a crew of two for only a few hours.

"Would someone please explain to me why we're not sending all eight of them up in Cardinal?" Regina Hartnell, a human factors engineer, spoke while leaning against the wall.

Timon glanced nervously at Colonel Gray, who had taken over management of the Mars program, making Timon his assistant. They worked together like the producer and director of a movie, with Timon as director, constantly fighting for artistic control of the final result. For Timon, artistic control meant no interference with the scientific goals of the mission. Morgan's discovery had already prompted revisions of those goals.

"Have you discussed this with your team?" the colonel asked Timon.

"Yes." Beads of sweat formed on Timon's dark forehead. "Remember, Regina, we can't bring the alien artifacts back unless we split up the team into two landers."

"I know that. I want to know why we're not giving priority to the safety of the entire Pax team."

"No team member is in danger," Timon said, his eye twitching. Sweat started to stain his armpits, even though the room temperature stayed at seventy degrees. He looked at Koll across the table, his eyes pleading. "Dr. Eriksen can explain."

"In the worst case," Koll said, looking around to address the entire room, "two team members might have to remain on Mars to catch the next ship home, if they still want to leave." Koll's first colony ship was scheduled to take off from Earth in three months. Now the first colonists might already be on Mars.

"You're going to strand them there?" Regina asked. The staff members standing around her looked shocked, but not the managers seated at the table. They gazed down at their papers. The military brass stared straight ahead as if they already knew what was going to happen and were waiting out the protest in the room. The laptop typing stopped.

Regina continued speaking, apparently not realizing or not caring that what she said next could damage her career. "Anything might happen out there in three months. They won't even have a doctor. What if the aliens return? We still don't know who they are or where they came from."

"The pilot and cosmonaut have plenty of supplies left in Pax and Rockhouse," Koll said. "And one of them has enough training to qualify as a medical officer." He deliberately avoided saying "Vlad" or "Diego" to make the conversation less emotional. "The crew's experiments proved that the habitat and power plant could support humans indefinitely, like the ones in the lunar colonies. The garden grows well in the greenhouse on Mars."

He stood to circle the table and look each person in the eye as he spoke with excitement about his vision. "The Pax team could be our first colonists, so we would have established our colony fifty-eight days ago instead of waiting three more months."

Colonel Gray and his staff, a man and woman on each side of him, continued looking straight ahead, as if they were sitting at attention. Some of the faces around the room displayed hostility, others disappointment or worry. The team managers looked resigned. None of them shared Koll's vision of the future of Mars exploration.

"Koll was describing the worst case," Timon said, his face expressionless and his shirt damp. "We'll do our best to get everyone on Pax II before it returns to Earth."

No one spoke for a while.

Then, in a voice that quelled further protest, the colonel said, "Possession of the artifacts is a matter of national security. If necessary, the two men can wait for another ride home." He and his staff members stood at the same time and marched out of the room.

Everyone else hurried back to their work without further discussion. Koll had sold his ideas to the lawmakers and financial backers, but his coworkers were not on board yet. None of them had volunteered to be colonists, which surprised him.

ॐॐॐ

The dust storm moved from Hellis Basin on the other side of Mars northeast toward Elysium Planitia. Watching its progress on her sleeve screen, Morgan hoped they could all take off before the full storm hit. Vlad and Diego drove her and the other astronauts to Cardinal for their flight into orbit. The clear, midday sky turned smoky when the storm started swirling up Ma'dim Vallis into Gusev Crater. On the ground they rode across, the rocks looked like broken seashells dusted with tangerine-colored talcum powder.

"How are you going to get to Pax if you can't see?" she asked Vlad from the passenger seat of the closed rover. The team had shut down Rockhouse, converted the lab into a self-watering greenhouse to keep their garden growing as long as possible, and set the power plant to continue operating automatically. Vlad and Diego planned to wait in the downed ship until time to leave. It was closer to Sparrow than Rockhouse was.

"We're going to drive very slowly and use our sonar navigators to avoid rocks."

"Oh," she said. "That should work."

ℯↄℯↄ

Visibility was less than one hundred meters when they reached Cardinal. As Morgan climbed carefully out of the rover and stepped onto the ground, dust flew between her suited legs and circled around them. Randy grabbed their flight bags from behind the rear seats. Everything else had already been loaded into Cardinal.

Michelle hugged Vlad goodbye, her helmet bumping his. He hung on as if he never wanted to let go. Morgan saw tears through his faceplate. She had expected him to give them a cheery sendoff. Was the big, strong Russian afraid of being left behind?

"Hurry," Cass said. "I want to take off before visibility gets below fifty meters."

They filed up the steps into Cardinal. Morgan let everyone go ahead of her so she could take time to keep her balance in the strong wind, which would have been a hurricane on Earth. She paused at the top to turn and wave at Vlad and Diego. They sat behind the wheels of their rovers waiting for Cardinal's departure, like taxi drivers who ferried tourists but never got to board the cruise ship. She could barely see the rocky ground beneath the gathering dust, which erased everything behind them, like Stephen King's Langoliers.

The camera above Morgan's head moved to point at the rovers. Cass must have been watching the monitor. "You two head for shelter, now," she said to the drivers. "We've got this covered. Morgan, get in here."

The rovers turned and drove off in tandem. When she lost sight of them through the opaque air, Morgan went inside and clambered over packages to the last empty seat, in the middle of the back row next to Randy. Artifacts and samples, securely tied, blocked the seat to her right. On her left, Randy steadied her until she settled next to him and strapped herself in. His helmet barely cleared the supplies attached to the ceiling. They would have no room to move around in the next eighteen hours, except to stand in front of their seats. Their elimination needs would strain the capacities of their spacesuits.

Aiden sat in front of Randy, where he watched Jamese enter data and check screens from the pilot's chair, beside Cass. Michelle buckled up next to Aiden, and more packages filled the seat to her right.

"Think I can't see you out there, stopped in the dust?" Cass asked Diego and Vlad over the radio while she flipped switches and checked electronic displays. "You know I have infrared sensors. All right, you can watch us take off, but then go straight to Pax."

"*Gracias, amante,*" Diego said. "*Hasta luego.*"

"So long," Vlad said with a catch in his voice. "Until we meet again." It sounded like a farewell toast, as if he didn't think he would see them for a very long time, if ever.

"The hatch is sealed," Jamese reported. "Morgan's hesitation delayed our departure by two minutes."

"We're going to start broadcasting to Earth now," Cass said, taking off her helmet. She glared at Jamese. "It's safe to remove yours now."

Morgan unfastened her helmet and attached it to the back of Michelle's seat. The lander design gave them plenty of leg room, like the crew cabin on Pax. Morgan wished the sky would clear so she could get a last look at the big ship on her arm screen as they left. The engines rumbled and roared until Morgan couldn't hear or feel anything else. She saw only reddish haze on the screen.

"Lift off," Jamese said.

"Adjust the flight angle," Cass said.

"Check," Jamese replied. "Now we're on trajectory for a perfect orbital insertion."

Morgan worried about how the G force on her abdomen might affect the baby. They had calculated it would be safe enough, but no pregnant woman had taken off from another planet, so how could they be sure?

"The pressure will not last long," Randy said.

They streaked out of the huge dust cloud. Morgan gasped when the force that pushed her against the seat finally let go. The pressure hadn't been as bad as when they left Earth, but she welcomed the return to microgravity, even though she had to remain strapped in until they reached orbit. The big forward screen showed a starry night sky in front of them.

Next to Morgan, Randy typed on his electronic notebook. After two months of intense activity, often working overtime on scheduled tasks, they had nothing else to do except wait for their ride home, stretch every two hours, and try not to get on each other's nerves in the cramped space.

Cardinal's orbital insertion went smoothly. Only the top of Olympus Mons showed clearly in the left viewport. Vlad and Diego would have to take off in the tiny lander during a planet-wide storm.

ഇൾൻ

Cassandra watched the angry orange curve of Mars roll by as she fidgeted in her seat. The message from Diego came three hours later than she expected.

"Cardinal, this is Pax."

Her body went limp with relief.

She flipped the broadcast switch and, remembering the huge audience, repressed most of what she wanted to say to him. "Pax, Cardinal here. What's your status?"

"Sparrow's team is secure in Pax." She groaned when he added, "We have lots of extra room for relaxing here. Do you feel like sardines yet?"

"Cardinal is orbiting as planned," Cassandra said. Then she flipped a switch and, to let him know the world would hear what he had just said, announced, "Ending the broadcast to Earth."

"*Chica*, you could have reminded me," Diego said. "I forgot you had to report when we arrived."

"Why did it take you so long?"

"We had to crawl through rock fields and find a way around the big boulders. Vlad almost sank his rover in a crater filled with dust."

"What's the visibility at ground level now?"

"Ten meters. I need to remove this gritty suit. Wish I could take yours off, too. Pax out."

"Wish you could. Cardinal out."

While Cassandra looked at the nearly featureless world below through her viewport, a seed of apprehension germinated into fear inside her. That storm was not going to subside before Pax II arrived. With nothing to do except think, she had begun to understand what the Mission Control plan had been all along.

"They're going to leave them on Mars," she said, unbuckling from her chair. She turned to face the crew as she floated up, her bulky suit jamming against the packages on the ceiling. Jamese looked up from her keyboard, her eyes wide.

Morgan shook her head. "No, they wouldn't do that on purpose."

"Pax, come in," Cassandra said. "Can you take off in this?"

"Say again." Diego's voice crackled from the interference of billions of tiny particles in the Martian atmosphere.

"How can you take off safely in the storm?" Cassandra asked.

"We can probably make it if the wind dies down a little."

"You're not sure?" She didn't like Diego's optimism, which often contradicted common sense and usually got him into trouble. "The wind's not going to die down in time. Put Vlad on."

"Good idea," Aiden said.

"Hello, Cardinal." Vlad's distorted, metallic voice came through the speaker. "I was just enjoying a warm shower."

"Enough needling." She didn't want to waste a second on small talk. "Do you think taking off in this storm is safe?"

"Safe?" Static broke up what he said next.

"I didn't catch your answer."

"It's not very safe, but what can Diego do? Pax II is due to make its orbital insertion in thirteen hours, and you have to get Morgan home before the baby is born."

"Hold on," Morgan said from the back row. "You're not going to risk your lives for me."

"What did she say?" Vlad asked. "Was that Morgan?"

"Yes," Cassandra said. "She doesn't want you to risk your lives to get her back sooner. She could have the baby on the ship, you know."

"Nobody knows if that works in microgravity," Vlad said.

"I don't think being in space will stop a birth," Randy said.

"Let me check something out with Mission Control," Cassandra said.

"All right. We'll listen to your broadcast."

She turned off the radio and pulled herself down to kneel backwards in her seat, her boots touching the console. "As soon as we finish unloading Cardinal into Pax II, I want to go down and get Diego and Vlad. Are you all with me on this?"

Everyone nodded except Jamese.

"What's your objection?" Cassandra asked, suppressing her annoyance at the unhappy woman who always disagreed, even in a life and death situation.

"The Cardinal tanks will be empty. You'll have to refuel and resupply the air and water from the tanks on Pax II."

"Yes. We'll replace them from the power plant."

"If Cardinal tips over again, or you don't make it back for some reason, our tanks won't be full when we leave."

The other woman's matter-of-fact tone spread cold around Cassandra's fear. Jamese's logic was correct, but it wasn't right.

"Why can't Diego and Vlad just wait out the dust storm and then fly up?" Jamese asked.

"Morgan needs to get back as soon as possible. We don't know how long the dust storm will last."

"So Morgan controls everything again."

Morgan's gloved hands held an abdomen that strained against her white spacesuit as she leaned back into her seat next to Randy. Cassandra had never seen her friend look so frightened.

"Jamese," Randy said. "Criticizing people is not helping us." He watched Morgan like a protective lover rather than a doctor.

"We have to be unanimous on this," Cassandra said, searching Jamese's dark eyes for agreement.

Jamese unfastened herself, rose, and turned to look around the cabin. Stars gleamed behind her through the right viewport. Everyone stared at her until she nodded. Cassandra flipped the broadcast switch.

"Mission Control, this is Cardinal. We have a concern about our crewmembers on the ground taking off in the dust storm. As you know, Sparrow isn't equipped to fly in extreme conditions. We recommend that I take Cardinal down to get them after the rest of the crew boards Pax II. Alternatively, we recommend orbiting in Pax II until the dust storm clears so that Sparrow can take off safely."

e∽ℰ∽ℑ

The cabin went silent, except for keyboard tapping and the rustling of people shifting in their seats, until the reply arrived from Mission Control nearly an hour later. "We considered your recommendation and decided to stay with the original plan. If the Sparrow pilot determines that flight conditions on the ground make the ascent too risky, the Sparrow crew can remain on Mars until the next ride home, in six months. You have a crewmember who needs to return to Earth immediately to prevent a life-threatening birth. Also, it is a matter of national security that you bring the alien artifacts to Earth as soon as possible."

Cassandra checked to make sure the broadcast switch was off before she spoke to the Cardinal crew again. "I already know it's too risky. I'm going to get them anyway. Jamese, you should inform Mission Control of my plan so that the rest of you don't ruin your careers. None of you should help me, either."

"You can't disobey a direct order," Jamese said. "They'll ask us to stop you."

Michelle looked up from typing on her notebook keypad and said, "Would you please wait to send your message? I am composing something to add to it."

"I want to add information, too," Randy said.

"Oh," Aiden said. "May I put in a few words?"

"All right," Jamese answered. "Just hurry up."

"Well, I'm not sure how to word this." Aiden tapped a letter at a time into his notebook with one finger.

Jamese's skin paled behind her red lips. "Why can't all of you just send separate messages?"

"You know that everyone can add to each broadcast if they want to," Morgan answered. "The Air Force didn't change that rule. I'm going to need time to write my part, probably until we dock."

"Then I won't be able to send the message until after we unload," Jamese said. "Cassandra could take off before Mission Control replies."

Morgan, Randy, Aiden, and Michelle nodded and smiled at Jamese.

"Thanks," Cassandra said as she returned to the radio. "Pax, this is Cardinal. Come in, Pax."

"*Hola*," Diego responded.

"I'm coming down in Cardinal to get you right after we dock with Pax II."

"Your voice is breaking up. Did you say you want to come back down here?" His voice cut out in places, but she could understand him.

"Yes. You are not, repeat, not to take off in that storm."

"I already decided Sparrow couldn't make it. Maybe we could wait out the worst part."

"Negative. Are you ready to say "I do"? My career will be over soon."

No reply came back over the radio for a while. Then Diego spoke. "No, *mi amor.* I will not allow it."

"I'm still commander of this mission, and I'll decide what's allowed. I want you to go to Rockhouse and wait for me there. Put Vlad on."

"Okay. *Gracias.*"

She knew Diego wanted her to come get him. They would have to use sonar technology to drive back to the power plant for refueling. She should land near the plant and have the men bring the rovers. Calculating how much time the refueling would take in the storm, she decided they could make it back before Pax II finished its first orbit, so they wouldn't delay the return to Earth. Why was Vlad taking so long?

When the radio crackled again, she wasn't prepared for Diego's news. "I can't find him."

"He's not on Pax?"

"No. I looked everywhere. He's not answering his suit radio, either, and the covered rover is gone."

CHAPTER 18

The fear inside Cassandra expanded into dread that tightened her chest as she turned toward the Cardinal crew again. Their faces reflected her anxiety. Why was Vlad driving around in the dust storm, not communicating? A cosmonaut who had already been to the moon and Mars wouldn't flip out under pressure. Maybe he didn't want to leave. She needed to find him, but how?

"I don't know why Vlad drove off," she said. "But he probably headed for Rockhouse."

"I agree," Randy said. "His action makes no sense. Even though he sneaked some vodka aboard Pax, he always obeyed orders that mattered. I think someone might have ordered him to stay at the last minute."

"You're right," Morgan said. "Vlad cried when he told us goodbye. I never saw him cry before."

"We need to tell Mission Control he deserted," Jamese said.

Cassandra stared at Jamese. "He's missing. That's all we know. Would you please send that message? Tell them I'm going back down in Cardinal to help find our lost crewmember."

Even Jamese grinned at that, along with the others. Maybe Cassandra wouldn't have to give up her career to rescue the men.

"How long until we rendezvous with Pax II?" she asked.

Jamese looked at her screen. "Two-and-a-half hours. The Pax II orbital insertion is in one hour. Mission Control just sent a message to confirm this. They want Sparrow to take off in three hours and dock. We should be on our way back to Earth before completion of the first orbit, so we can use Mars to slingshot into our interplanetary trajectory."

"Well, we're going to have to make an extra orbit," Cassandra said. "Is everyone okay with that?"

As they all nodded agreement, Jamese added, "As long as we're not disobeying an order."

☙☙☙

No one had heard from Vlad forty-five minutes later, when the response to Jamese's message came back from Mission Control: "Cardinal, we considered your latest recommendation. Colonel Gray's orders are to stay with the original plan. For national security, it is imperative that we have no delay in returning the artifacts. We need to know as soon as possible who else has been in our solar system, when, and why. Your pilot and cosmonaut would want to do their duty for the people of Earth and stay behind if they cannot meet the schedule. They can come back on the next ship."

Cassandra turned toward the crew, but before she could talk, Jamese said, "I'm sorry, but we can't allow you to return to the surface. If I have to, I'll relieve you of command. Don't let your feelings for Diego interfere with your judgment."

"Please speak only for yourself," Michelle said. "Can we not discuss this?"

"I don't take orders from the Air Force, and I won't leave anyone behind," Cassandra said.

"We need to work as a team here," Randy said.

"I'll go back down with Cassandra," Aiden said.

Morgan grabbed a container from the pile of samples on the seat next to her and moved toward the air lock. "If these artifacts are more important than people's lives, I'll toss out all the containers."

Jamese lunged at Morgan over the head of Michelle, who had her seat straps fastened.

Cassandra had not intended to lose control. She needed to reestablish her authority so that she could bring Diego and Vlad back. "Please stay in your seats and don't toss anything out yet." Morgan and Jamese did as she asked. "Thanks for your support, but this one's on me. I won't let any of you risk your career or stop me from going to get our crewmembers." She waved her hand around the cabin as she spoke a warning to Jamese. "If you decide to take over this ship or Pax II, you'll be risking a mutiny charge."

Ignoring Cassandra, Jamese typed rapidly on her keyboard.

Cassandra turned back to the console to radio Diego. "Any contact with Vlad yet?"

"Nothing."

"Well, I have some good news."

"¿Qué pasa?"

"The wedding is on."

"They won't let you come down here to help find Vlad?"

"No. If they think that stuff is more important than your lives, I don't want to be part of them anymore. I'll be down as soon as we unload."

ᏇᏇᏇ

Pax II arrived on schedule. After its orbital insertion, it gradually caught up to Cardinal. Everyone put their helmets back on, a safety precaution, before they docked with the return ship. Morgan could see Pax II through the front left viewport.

"Broadcasting to Earth," Cass announced. "Docking procedure initiated."

Her muscles tense, Morgan concentrated on breathing normally until she could board Pax II. It had plenty of oxygen, water, and food, plus room to move around. Randy put his gloved hand over hers.

Cass went through all the checks with Jamese and then said, "Docking complete. Ending broadcast."

Morgan's body was so stiff after being confined to her seat area for eighteen hours that she didn't know if she could make it through the air lock without help. She stood in her thick spacesuit and stretched, her boots attached to the floor by Velcro, as she had done every two hours while they waited for the big ship. The stretching didn't help much. She would have to push off and try to float through the hatches without bumping into anything. The others were already unloading flight bags and supply containers. She grabbed an armload of artifacts to carry into Pax II.

Randy took them from her. "After the ordeal of waiting in orbit, you need to rest for a while," he ordered. "We can handle the unloading. You need your arms free until you get used to navigating in microgravity again."

"But I haven't been doing anything for hours. I want to do my share of the unloading so Cass can take off faster."

"Sorry," Randy told her, pulling her gently by both arms toward the open air lock. "My orders are to put you straight to bed."

"Go with him," Cass said. "We've got this."

Morgan was not happy that they were coddling her again, on orders from Earth. She wished they would just let her do her part, but she went with Randy to avoid causing a problem that might delay Cass. She really did want to be alone in her room for a while. The baby started kicking.

At the docked hatch, Jamese waited her turn to go through behind Aiden, her arms full of samples.

"Excuse us, please," Randy said. "Medical priority."

Jamese frowned at Morgan but backed away.

Morgan felt a rush of relief when she reached the safety of Pax II and removed her helmet. Soon she would be taking a nap in clean clothes. She wished Cass could do the same.

ananan

Cassandra hoped Vlad was still alive, but she had to get to Diego first. Why had she even considered delaying their marriage because of this job? She hoped it wasn't too late for them to be together and raise a family.

"Mission Control, this is Pax II," she reported. "Docking is complete. Unloading from Cardinal to Pax II is underway. Mission Specialist Kim will give you details."

While Jamese continued the report and Michelle and Aiden unloaded the rest of the containers, Cassandra loaded the extra air, water, and fuel tanks from Pax II into Cardinal. Jamese looked irritated, but in the broadcast she mentioned only the samples and artifacts they were unloading. No one talked about Cassandra's actions as she started loading supplies that she and the men still on Mars would need to make it back to Pax II.

After Aiden took the last container off Cardinal, Cassandra said, "Unloading is complete. Now I'm performing a manual undocking and returning for our remaining crewmembers.

The Sparrow pilot has determined that the small lander cannot take off safely in the dust storm. I plan to land near Rockhouse by instruments for refueling and resupplying. Pilot Garcia can meet me there and help search for Mission Specialist Kolovna." By the time her message reached Earth, the Air Force wouldn't be able to stop her. She disconnected the remote control equipment.

Switching off the broadcast, she continued transmitting only to Diego. "I'm coming to get you, baby."

"*Gracias.* Vlad hasn't returned yet."

"He might be at Rockhouse. Meet me there as soon as you can. Take as much time as you need to drive safely through the storm."

"Okay."

She changed the transmission settings to include Pax II. "Undocking Cardinal now."

Jamese's voice came over the radio, "Cardinal, I recommend against that unauthorized maneuver. I'm broadcasting your transmission to Earth and taking remote control of Cardinal."

Cassandra had counted on Jamese's reaction, which would prevent Mission Control from blaming anyone except Cassandra for her rescue trip. She had already blocked the ship pilot option, so she continued the undocking procedure and pulled slowly away from Pax II. "Separation is complete."

"Cardinal, please restore your remote control facility and return to Pax II," Jamese said. "If you should need assistance, we would have to control Cardinal from here."

"Entering Mars atmosphere," Cassandra said. "Communications might be difficult through the dust storm. Visibility is fifty percent."

"Cassandra Nickels, you left your command post and disobeyed a direct order from Mission Control. As ranking astronaut on board Pax II, I'm assuming command of this mission. Return at once."

Cassandra didn't respond. As soon as she brought Diego and Vlad back to Pax II, she would straighten out who was in command. Right now she needed to watch her instrument readings closely to make the most difficult landing anyone had ever attempted. Cardinal vibrated as it arced down toward the surface, through dust so thick the viewports and screen remained blank. Cassandra reminded herself that this would be like a simulator landing without the fake visuals—no problem for her. She preferred landing by instruments.

℃つ℃つ

Morgan kept her radio on while she rested against her navy blue bedspread, dressed in extra-large gray shorts, T-shirt, and socks. A white net cover, fastened to the bed frame, kept her from floating off.

When she heard Jamese assume command, Morgan unfastened the cover and floated out of her room. She used the handrails in the hall to pull herself along faster, taking care not to bump her large belly against a wall. Jamese wasn't going to be in command very long. After Morgan shoved herself through the crew cabin door, Randy, Aiden, and Michelle followed, all wearing shorts, tees, and socks.

In the front left seat, the commander's chair, Jamese turned to face them, still in her thermal undergarment. "Please continue with your rest period. I can handle this."

"You'll handle nothing," Morgan said, her cheeks warming. "Michelle is in command. She has more experience than you."

Michelle looked around at everyone in surprise. Randy and Aiden nodded at her. Morgan hoped the shy Frenchwoman would take her rightful place.

"This is a United States spacecraft," Jamese said, her face a cold, beautiful mask. "An American should be in command."

"Morgan is right," Michelle said, in a stronger voice than she normally used. "This is an international mission. I must assume command of this ship until our mission commander returns."

"According to our regulations," Jamese said, smiling grimly, "our commander has deserted her ship. She is no longer in command of this mission. You can't command an American ship."

"Yes, she can," Morgan said. "Michelle was born on American soil, while her parents were vacationing in New York, so she has dual citizenship."

"What?" Jamese's cool exterior cracked into sudden fury. She flipped the broadcast switch off and moved into the aisle, blocking access to the two front chairs and control panel. "That's not true," she said. "I would have known. Even if it is, Cassandra is no longer in command."

"It is true," Michelle said softly. "Please move so I can pilot the ship."

Jamese didn't budge. "The ship doesn't need any piloting to orbit the planet."

"Come on," Randy said. "We need to work together."

"Let's check on Cassandra," Aiden said.

"She's still commander unless Mission Control removes her," Morgan said. "You don't have the authority to do that without our agreement."

Jamese shoved past them down the center aisle. "You can take over for an hour or so, Michelle, until Mission Control receives Cassandra's transmission and returns the order to put me in command. I need to change, anyway." She zoomed over the seat tops and out of the crew cabin.

"Starting retro-rockets," Cass's voice crackled over the radio. "Adjusting for three-hundred-mile-an-hour winds. Visibility is near zero."

Michelle slid into the commander's chair and enlarged the radar screen that showed the Cardinal blip. "Pax II copies you," she said. "Good luck."

Morgan stared out the viewport. The others crowded in front of the seat behind Michelle to watch the screen. Sandwiched between Randy on her left and Aiden on her right, Morgan forced herself not to hold her breath while Cass landed. She didn't want the baby to be short of oxygen.

"Coming down slower and slower. Almost there," Cass said. "Touchdown. I can't see anything here."

CHAPTER 19

Diego watched the sonar readout on his helmet screen while his rover crawled through the moaning storm, unable to see anything beyond his faceplate. He wished the rover seats were enclosed so that he wouldn't feel the wind pushing and pulling at him, like some Martian *diablo*. Every time the outline of a large object appeared in the readout, he had to steer around it and then use the longitude and latitude readouts of Cardinal's location from Pax II to adjust his direction. Because of the swirling dust, the readouts often flickered.

His back, shoulders, and head ached from the constant vigilance and redirection. Would he be lost in the storm on this strange world forever—in purgatory with no way out? Cassi, who was his only hope, waited for him like a beacon as her voice marked the trail back to Rockhouse in his readout.

"You're halfway here," Cassi said over the radio.

He kept driving toward the coordinates of that voice, around boulder after boulder, and over the smaller ones.

"Can you go faster?" she asked. "When Pax II reaches the other side of Mars, we'll lose our navigation."

"I can try, but the rocks block my way."

"Hurry."

"I speed to your side." He pressed the fuel pedal harder and felt the rover rise and fall as it drove over larger boulders. "If I don't make it in time, go back safely, and remember that I love you."

"I'm not leaving without you. You'd better pay attention and not flip that thing over. I don't want to have to come looking for you on foot."

"*Si, señorita.*"

He checked the readout, went around another boulder, and then readjusted his direction. He wanted to turn off the audio feed from the atmosphere to shut out the moaning wind, but he needed to hear the rover engine.

"Any sign of Vlad?" he asked.

"No. The other rover is not at Rockhouse. We need yours to refuel Cardinal."

Diego's stomach churned. If he didn't make it back to Rockhouse, Cassi would be stranded there. If he did make it back, they would have to leave his Russian friend behind. They couldn't search for him in this storm, and Pax II couldn't wait to leave until the storm passed because it might rage on for weeks. Maybe Vlad had found a sheltered place to set up the portable habitat, which they had stowed in his rover.

As Diego zigzagged through the buffeting, wailing darkness, the latitude and longitude readout disappeared. Pax II must have orbited to the other side of Mars. Now he was blind.

"Which way should I go?"

"Straight ahead," Cassi said. "You're almost here. Just a few hundred more meters. I'm coming to meet you."

"What? How are you coming to meet me?" He wondered if Vlad had arrived in the other rover.

"Before Pax II went behind Mars, I tied all the ropes I could find together, secured one end to Rockhouse, and put the other end around my waist. I'm about two hundred meters from the air lock. Keep driving in the same direction."

"Go back, Cassi. The ropes might come apart. You would be lost."

"I know how to tie knots. Just drive. That's an order."

"I thought you quit."

"I'm still your ground commander."

"Yes, ma'am."

Diego concentrated on driving straight and slow, so he could find her without running her down. The sonar readout showed a boulder in front of him, but the shape of the rock kept changing, as if it were swaying in the wind. He must be hallucinating. Even in a dust storm, the winds of Mars weren't strong enough to move boulders.

He didn't know if he was still heading toward Cassi, and he had to go around the boulder. He could miss her by a yard and keep driving in the storm until his fuel ran out. When he was almost on top of the big rock, he stopped. It glowed in front of him.

"I think I'm losing my mind. This rock is moving and radiating some kind of light. If I go around it, I don't know if I can find you."

"It's not a rock. You almost ran over me. I hung glow sticks around my neck, arms, and legs."

"*Gracias, mi amor.* You saved me."

"Don't get excited yet. We still have to follow this rope back to Rockhouse." She climbed in, holding their lifeline, and tried to wrap her spacesuited arms around him.

He pulled her suit torso against his to return the hug. "Let me thank you properly when we get back."

"Please do, my fiancé." She pulled away. "But now, if we don't refuel fast, Pax II will finish its second orbit and leave without us. To Rockhouse."

Diego went back to his unending task of driving. He inched the rover along while Cassi coiled the rope hand over hand beside him. Skirting the big rocks was no longer a problem because they had the rope to lead them back. Rockhouse finally appeared on his sonar readout. Their Martian home grew larger and larger until they arrived at the rover port, which stood empty. Where was Vlad? Diego's arms and legs were numb from the effort to get there.

"We have to go," Cassi said. "I secured a line from here to Cardinal and from there to the power plant. You can rest after we refill the tanks and take off."

"Just the sight of you is all the rest I need," he said.

ⱸↄⱸↄ

His stomach muscles tight with anxiety, Koll kept careful notes in his workspace on the lighted conference table while the argument in the room played itself out.

Colonel Gray and his staff sat at one end of the table, Timon and his NASA managers at the other. Koll sat on Timon's left, attending as future director of the first Martian colony.

The results of this meeting could determine whether or not the colony was already established. If it was, he could walk out of here with a promotion. He hoped it would come with the blessing of Timon, who was still Mars Program Director. Koll needed his support to get the Mission Control team behind the colonization project.

"I know Commander Nickels disobeyed an order," Timon was saying. "But she is authorized to override orders from Earth when the lives of her crewmembers are in danger." Timon's left eye twitched. "None of the Air Force directives has rescinded that authorization."

"Consider it rescinded now." Colonel Gray pounded the table. "Pax II must return the artifacts as soon as its orbital position allows." The big screen behind him showed a simulation of the spacecraft's elliptical path around the hazy red globe.

"They can leave Mars orbit in nine hours," Timon said, the twitches increasing around his eye.

He was getting angry, Koll thought, his stomach cramping as Timon continued.

"Commander Nickels and Pilot Garcia can refuel and dock with Pax II before then, but they won't have time to search for Cosmonaut Kolovna. If we could have the ship complete one or two more orbits, they might be able to find him."

"Can they refuel in the dust storm?" the colonel asked.

"Yes. They have the technology to do that."

"Perhaps we should reassign command to Mission Specialist Kim." The colonel stood, walked to the screen, and jabbed a finger at the current position of Pax II. "A Frenchwoman is piloting our spacecraft just because she happened to be born in New York."

"Commander Nickels acted in accordance with her training and orders." Frowning, Timon passed his left hand over the twitching eye. "I recommend that she retain command and we inform the crew that the authorization to override orders is rescinded."

Colonel Gray nodded. "All right, Director Brown, provided she returns to Pax II within nine hours." He slapped the screen. "No additional orbits." Turning to Koll, the colonel asked, "Can the cosmonaut survive in that storm?"

Koll cleared his throat, searching his mind for the most diplomatic response possible. He didn't want to further antagonize Timon, who watched Koll like an angry ant waiting to be stepped on. An eye twitch dislodged a bead of sweat that rolled down Timon's cheek.

"Vladimir Kolovna is in excellent health and has advanced survival skills," Koll said, hoping his anxiety wasn't apparent.

Timon relaxed in his chair. His eye stopped twitching.

"Then we must assume that he will survive unless we determine otherwise," Colonel Gray said. His aides nodded approval. "Apparently the Russians ordered him to stay behind so they could claim the colony."

Timon lifted his hand in objection but then lowered it without speaking.

"Dr. Eriksen, can the Russians claim the colony?" Colonel Gray asked while scowling at Timon.

Koll had been waiting for this question. He stood, multiplied a document on his table screen, and shoved the copies to everyone around the lighted table. Then he looked at Timon, who nodded, his face resigned. With this tentative approval, Koll released his internal tension and answered the colonel.

"I don't think they can claim it. This document is the United Nations agreement on the establishment of colonies on extraterrestrial bodies." Koll read from it. "The sponsorship of a colony is determined by the citizenship of the person who first sets foot on the colony soil."

"The colony isn't established yet," Timon said.

Koll multiplied another document next to the U.N. agreement, his stomach cramps returning. "Here is my recommendation to establish Gusev Colony as the first colony on Mars, with the United States of America as sponsor. Morgan Zeller, an American citizen, first set foot on the crater when she rescued the original Cardinal crew. Occupation of the living quarters in the crater has been continuous since that time, so the establishment of the colony can be retroactive to the date she arrived, according to the international agreement. If the Russian stays, he can continue the occupation for the United States until our next ship arrives because he was part of the original landing party."

Colonel Gray sat and looked at the table. Koll sat down too. Silence filled the room as the colonel read the documents. His aides and the NASA managers did the same. Timon's eye resumed twitching.

"What if the Russian left the crater?" Colonel Gray asked.

"That's unlikely," Koll replied, his stomach in knots now. This had to go well, or the colony might never be approved. "Vlad needs the habitat or the downed ship—which is also part of the colony—to survive. If he has left, we would need to reestablish the colony when the next ship arrives. He is probably waiting out the storm in the rover, not far from Pax, or in the emergency lander. The pilot reported that the cosmonaut took extra oxygen and supplies with him, but the rover fuel tank was not full."

Colonel Gray rose and reached out across the table. "Dr. Eriksen, it is time to assume your position as colony director, reporting to me."

"Yes, sir." Without a glance at Timon, who must have been furious, Koll stood, walked to the head of the table, and shook Colonel Gray's hand.

While the colonel and his staff marched out of the conference room, Timon sat with a hand over his eye. The rest of his face looked blank as he and his managers gathered their papers and rose to leave.

"Timon, I didn't know this was going to happen now," Koll said, returning to his seat. The other NASA managers looked surprised. It wasn't really a lie because he didn't know the colonel was going to remove the colony from Timon's control. Guilt filled Koll anyway.

"You certainly were prepared for it." Still holding his eye, Timon shook Koll's hand. "Congratulations, Director Eriksen. Thanks for the copies of your reports."

A heaviness settled in Koll's chest. "I would have given them to you before the meeting, but it was called in such a hurry, and the reports just came in."

"Uh-huh," Timon said, removing his hand from his face to reveal slight contempt.

"When you have time," Koll said. "I'd like to discuss the colony plans with you."

"Later. We need to get those people safely off the planet first."

Timon strode away, leaving Koll to finish collecting stray papers from the conference table. As everyone left, no one else looked at him. He wanted to be excited about his new appointment, but he just felt bad that the rest of the staff was not enthused about it.

ᔖᓬᔖ

Morgan couldn't relax until Cass and Diego returned to Pax II. She sat strapped into the pilot's chair, on Michelle's right, and waited for another transmission from the surface. Randy floated by, handed out MREs to everyone for lunch, and went back to his seat. Jamese stalked up the aisle, her Velcro boots ripping from the floor with each step, and then leaned over Morgan to check the communications display.

"Any response from Earth yet?"

"I think it's coming in now."

"Finally. Get ready to move over, Michelle."

"Pax II, this is Mission Control. Prepare to leave at completion of your next orbit, in eight hours. We confirm the status of Payload Specialist Michelle Dushay as Pax II commander until the return of Mission Commander Nickels."

"What?" Jamese screeched, her face reddening with rage.

Morgan leaned forward to hear the rest.

"Cosmonaut Vladimir Kolovna is assumed lost in the storm but probably still alive. Tell the Cardinal crew to leave the surface as soon as refueling is complete. Their authority to override orders in life-threatening situations is hereby rescinded. The cosmonaut's duty now is to continue the Gusev Colony, which was established by Morgan Zeller for the United States of America. Good luck to all of you."

"No way," Jamese yelled, her face nearly the shade of her painted lips. She pulled at Morgan's arm. "That can't be right. We landed before you did, and Cassandra disobeyed orders. Get up and let me send another message."

"Let go of her," Randy ordered, jumping toward the front of the crew cabin.

Morgan's ears throbbed from the loud voices. She tried to pry Jamese's fingers from her forearm while Michelle pushed Jamese back. Randy and Aiden, floating above, tugged at her shoulders. Jamese's boots tore loose from the floor. Her body shot back and up, knocking the men into the ceiling.

"This is assault," she said as she disentangled herself from them.

"Please, send your message, but don't attack me," Morgan said, floating up to leave the front seat. She couldn't get past Randy and Aiden. The radio crackled.

"Come in, Pax II," Diego said.

Morgan pulled herself down in front of the radio again and told Jamese, "That message can wait a minute." She looked at Michelle, who nodded, and then answered Diego, "We copy you, Cardinal. What's your status?"

"Refueling is half done." His voice cut out, but Morgan heard the question. "How much longer?"

"About eight hours until we leave orbit. Can you finish in time to dock and get on board?"

"Yes, but we need more time to look for Vlad."

"Mission Control told us to leave him. Please put Cass on."

"*Sí.* Here she is."

"…air full of dirt…can't find him anyway."

"I only got part of that. Can you hear me?"

"Yes."

"You have to take off as soon as you refuel. The Air Force took away your authority to override orders but left you in command of the mission."

"…pull my strings…"

"Hurry," Morgan said. "Pax II out." Michelle patted her arm. She picked up the rest of her lunch and let Jamese take the pilot's seat. Randy winked at Morgan, and Aiden waved a high five as she made her way to the back row. The baby turned inside her. She needed to calm down. Cass and Diego would probably be all right, and maybe Vlad would, too.

"Mission Control, this is Mission Specialist Kim," Jamese said, beginning her broadcast. "Please clarify your previous message. The original Cardinal crew landed on Mars before Morgan Zeller."

While Jamese droned on, Morgan fell asleep in her comfortable chair.

ⲉⲥⲉⲥ

The tinny sound of Cass's voice over the radio woke Morgan.

"Pax II…Cardinal…finished refueling…we're ready to take off."

So Vlad was still missing. After nearly an hour of sleep, she felt better, but her bladder was full.

Still in the pilot's chair, Jamese replied to Cass, "Pax II reads you, Cardinal. We're ready to bring you up on autopilot."

"Negative," Cass said. "Please stand by in case we need help."

"You can't take off manually in such low visibility," Jamese said.

"This is hard enough without your objections. Stand by."

"Be right back," Morgan said. She hurried out of the crew cabin, wishing she could have waited until Cardinal docked.

When she returned, Aiden sat in the pilot's chair, discussing flight data with Michelle and Cass. Jamese sulked in the back row.

"What happened?" Morgan whispered as she sat by Randy, behind Michelle.

"Cassandra requested a different pilot," Randy said with a grin. "I need to go do my job, though. Excuse me."

He climbed around Morgan, sat by Jamese, and began talking softly to her. Morgan knew he was responsible for the mental stability of the crew, but she felt jealous when he left her to help Jamese. Then Morgan regretted being so childish. She needed to focus on Cardinal's safe return.

"Coming up through the atmosphere…instrument readouts," Cass reported.

"Adjusting our pitch," Diego added.

As Morgan looked out the right viewport, all she saw was reddish fuzz. She stood to check Michelle's screen and watched the point where Cardinal should leave the Martian atmosphere.

"Everything looks okay on the screens," Cass said. "We should break through in a few minutes."

Morgan tried to ignore the low hum of voices from the back row, where Randy and Jamese talked on. Why wasn't he watching for Cass and Diego with the rest of them? She kept her eyes on Mars, straining to see a speck of light. Finally, she detected a bright pinpoint on the round edge of the rusty tapestry. She couldn't help calling out, "Randy, I see them."

He rushed over to the viewport, leaning into her side to see over her head. The pleasure of his closeness mixed with joy at her friends' safe departure from the planet and sorrow for the crewmate left behind. Randy hugged her.

"We see you, Pax II, and the stars," Cass said. "We can see again."

"You're coming in clearly," Aiden said. "Pax II is ready for docking procedures as soon as you match our orbit."

Michelle turned and smiled at everyone. Morgan and Randy smiled back. Aiden grinned as he got up and went back to Jamese, who was not smiling. He took her hand in his and said, "Come sit near me."

"No thanks."

A message arrived from Mission Control.

Pax II, NASA affirms Morgan Zeller as the first colonist and Cassandra Nickels as the mission commander. The president would like to speak to both of them right after you leave Mars orbit.

"Bullshit," Jamese said. She launched herself out of the crew cabin, muttering more obscenities.

Aiden looked sad but not hurt as he returned to the pilot's chair. He and Michelle talked with Cass during her approach.

Then Cass said the words Morgan had been waiting to hear all day, "Ready for docking."

After Cass and Diego completed the docking procedure, everyone except Jamese stood near the air lock to welcome their commander and pilot. In an hour Pax II would leave for Earth.

CHAPTER 20

On the surface of Mars, Vlad waited and listened inside Sparrow. The small lander ran out of oxygen. He secured his helmet and set it to block outside sounds so he could pick up the radio transmissions from Pax II as clearly as possible. He would have to stop at the original Pax to wait out the storm and refill his tanks before returning to Rockhouse. He had to stay in Sparrow until he was certain that Cardinal would not come back for him. After he heard the words "docking procedure complete," he went out through the air lock.

Vlad wished he could return to Earth with his crew. He could not because his duty to Mother Russia was clear. He would try to claim Gusev Colony, but the Americans would not let the Russians have it. He would refuel Sparrow and fly it beyond Gusev to found a new colony. How much better it would have been if the entire crew could have stayed and lived here together, without this squabbling over colonies. Also, he might have had a chance for happiness with Michelle.

Swaying in the wind, he felt for the hatch handle to turn and lock it. Then he grabbed the rails, lumbered down the steps, and followed a rope from the bottom step to where he had left the rover. He couldn't see anything except the sonar readout of the vehicle against the top of his visor. Hand over hand, struggling through the flying dirt, he made it to a mound of sand.

Using his long arms, Vlad scraped away most of the sand. The other end of the rope ended at a huge thermal blanket that covered the rover. Leaving the rope attached, he tried to fold the blanket, but the wind kept pulling the edges out of his gloves. He had to hurry before the rover was covered in dust again, so he bunched up the cover until he could get his arms around the blanket, stowed it in the rear cabinet, and then un-fastened the rope. It whipped around furiously in the storm, striking his arms. However, the lashes merely felt like nudges through his spacesuit.

Vlad wrestled the rope into a coil and stowed it. He climbed into the rover and started his slow crawl to Pax I through the boulders and craters, which were visible only on his helmet's sonar screen. He left his helmet on and did not fill the rover cabin with air, to conserve it. At Pax I, he would make his futile announcement about claiming the colony, after Pax II started toward Earth.

"Preparing to leave orbit," Cassandra said over his suit radio.

Grateful for the company of the occasional transmissions from Pax II, he kept his send function on mute so no one would hear him clear his throat or cough.

Cass continued. "I'm starting the engines so we can move toward the interplanetary trajectory, now."

He drove on in the wild nothingness. The realization that he was alone on Mars, without any orbiting human beings who could come down and rescue him, made it difficult to breathe. He hoped he was alone. How long ago did those aliens get here? Or were they native Martians? His breaths came in ragged gasps. He glanced at his arm to check the oxygen supply in the electronic readout but couldn't see it. Vlad stopped the rover, not sure where he was going. He had to think.

No, he couldn't stop. The sand would cover the rover and bury him in it. He started the motor again. Then he used his tongue to flip a switch that transferred the suit readout to the bottom of his visor, below the sonar display that the rover fed him. He watched the display carefully for boulders and craters but didn't see any big ones directly ahead. The oxygen level in the readout was much lower than it should be. The tank must be leaking slowly through a tiny hole. He reached under the seat for his spare tank, his last one. With one hand, he carefully removed the punctured tank and stowed it under the seat to repair later.

While he was connecting the spare tank, the rover tipped slightly to the side. It stopped and wouldn't go forward. He checked the sonar display again and saw the image of a small crater surrounding the back left wheel. Stuck. He would have to get out and pry the wheel loose.

"Mission Control, we have achieved our interplanetary trajectory," Cassandra said over the radio. "We'll see you in three months. Pax II out."

Vlad held back tears of loneliness. He didn't need extra moisture clogging his ventilation system.

He got out and stumbled through the shoving wind toward the back. Slipping, he grabbed the tether attached to his leg ring and followed it to the back of the rover. Then he felt around the bottom of the left rear wheel. It rested inside the crumbling edge of a small crater.

Grabbing a handhold on the rover, he stood, knees aching, opened a cabinet behind the wheel, and pulled out a long, flat piece of hard plastic. He climbed into the tiny crater and pushed one end of the plastic under the huge, trapped tire as hard as he could. After scooping out some of the sand that was filling his seat, he climbed back into the rover, closed the door, and tromped on the fuel pedal. The tire rolled up onto the plastic slab, out of the hole. He stopped again to retrieve the slab and put it away. Then he resumed his snail's journey toward the shelter of the big ship.

A transmission from Earth reached him. "Pax II, this is President Cole. First, I want to commend Commander Cassandra Nickels for her brave rescue of Pilot Diego Garcia. Next, I extend congratulations from the American people, the lunar colonies, the International Space Station, and the United Nations to Mission Specialist Morgan Zeller as the first Martian colonist. Our congratulations to the entire Pax crew for founding the first colony on Mars. The United States government is honored to sponsor the Gusev Colony. After you return to Earth, please plan to visit the White House with your families for a dinner in your honor. And Ms. Zeller, good luck with the impending birth of your child. I almost had my last one in a taxi, but nobody has ever raced to the hospital in a spaceship. I wish all of you a safe journey home."

Vlad chuckled. He was glad to hear the recognition for Morgan. The Americans had already claimed the colony, so he didn't need to hurry to make his claim. The sonar picture of Pax I grew and grew on his display, welcoming him to what had been his home for three months, the place that would save his life now. He had only one-quarter tank of oxygen left when he reached the grounded ship.

Going inside was like entering a paradise. Activation of the air lock turned on the emergency lights and started up the life support systems. As soon as he wiped the dust from his visor, he could see again. He set the helmet to receive outside sound and enjoyed the purring of the air conditioning unit. In a few minutes, he could remove his helmet and smell something besides his own body odors. Then he could broadcast his announcement.

�℘✄✠

In the conference room at KSC, when Koll heard the English translation of the Russian announcement, he hoped Timon would lend support to the colony project. "Cosmonaut Vladimir Kolovna sends us the following message from Mars," the translator said. "Greetings to my shipmates on Pax II, my Russian comrades, and all people on Earth, in the lunar colonies, and on the International Space Station. As the first permanent inhabitant of Gusev Colony, I claim it for Russia. My country is sending more colonists to make their home on Mars soon. With approval from the Russian government, you are welcome to visit our colony in peace at any time."

Mild laughter erupted around the long conference table.

"Well, they had to try," Koll said.

Timon and his staff stopped smiling.

"What do you think Cosmonaut Kolovna will do?" Colonel Gray asked.

"You know the cosmonauts better than I do, Director Brown," Koll said, turning toward Timon, who sat near the other end of the table.

Timon cleared his throat and looked at Colonel Gray. "Sir, I think Vlad will leave Gusev Crater to disestablish our colony and found a Russian colony somewhere else."

"Where?"

"The most likely place, I think, is Cydonia."

Koll wished Timon would make eye contact with him, but the Mars director continued looking at Colonel Gray, with no expression on his face.

"Given that we have proof of an alien visit to Mars, the Russians would probably want to determine whether the landforms in Cydonia could be the remains of an alien encampment."

"Can he get that far?"

"Yes, if he takes the lander back up to orbit first. He might try to establish a colony close to our power plant and habitat, though, so he can keep getting fuel and supplies. I think—"

"Excuse me, gentlemen," Koll said, looking at his table screen. "A message just arrived about the Russians."

Timon stopped talking and stared at his own screen, without even a glance in Koll's direction.

"Go on," Colonel Gray said.

The NASA managers and Air Force personnel around the table shifted in their seats. Those standing or sitting in chairs around the walls leaned forward to hear the news.

"A Russian supply ship is nearing Mars. Our intelligence says that it carries a power plant, habitat, and rovers to land at Cydonia."

A NASA staff member came into the room and delivered a printed message to Timon. He read the paper without any expression then stood. "Please excuse me and my staff. We have an urgent matter to attend to."

"Is there a problem on Pax II?" Colonel Gray asked.

"Yes."

"Please share your information with us, Director Brown."

"It's classified."

"We all have top secret clearance."

"One of the crew might be suffering a mental breakdown."

"Which one?"

Timon's right eye twitched. "Colonel, this is a personnel matter—"

"Everything about this mission is my concern. A mental breakdown could affect the safe return of the alien artifacts. Which crewmember?"

"Mission Specialist Jamese Kim. I really need to go, sir."

"First, fill me in on what happened."

"She has withdrawn to her quarters and will not communicate with anyone."

"Are any of the artifacts stored in her quarters?"

"We don't know. If you would please let us—"

"Have her quarters searched and place a guard outside her door."

Timon stiffened and shot a pleading look at Koll, the first acknowledgment all morning that they were on the same team.

"Sir," Koll said. "If the NASA team could have a few hours to assess the situation and make a recommendation before they take action, I will keep you informed about every detail."

The colonel stood and looked around the room. Several heads nodded at him. "Very well. But I want some resolution by the end of the day." He left the room, followed by his staff.

While NASA managers scooped their papers and equipment off the conference table and hurried out, Timon walked around the chairs to shake Koll's hand. "Thank you," he said with extreme politeness. "Please join us in the control room while we resolve this situation."

"I'm glad to help," Koll said with a smile.

Unsmiling, Timon nodded and left. Even though he had enlisted Koll's support as a last resort, it was progress. Maybe the director would look at the plans for the colony later, but he still seemed distant.

CHAPTER 21

"P lease open the door so we can talk," Randy said as he hovered next to Jamese's room. He tried the handle again, but it remained locked. She had not come out for breakfast again. He pulled his notepad from his back pocket and checked the medical sensors. Her vital signs were good, and she was conscious. He sent her a message. "Are you feeling all right? Would you like some medication?"

The door opened. Jamese grabbed his arm, knocking the notepad loose into the air, and pulled him into her room. "Would you please leave me alone?" she asked through clenched teeth.

"I cannot." Randy twisted his arm out of her grip. "You know that. You are exhibiting irrational behavior."

She crossed her arms and folded her legs above her bed, like a levitating yogi preparing to meditate. "What's irrational about wanting to be alone?"

"You are withdrawing from the team, which is not healthy. You have not eaten with us all week."

She reached behind her back and slid open a cabinet door to reveal shelves filled with food and drink packages. "I prefer eating alone."

"What about showering and grooming?"

"The bathroom is less crowded while all of you are sleeping. Do I smell bad to you? Is that why you don't want me?"

"I want to be your friend."

She turned her back on him. "I don't need any more friends. I have lots of friends on Earth."

He reached out and touched her shoulder. "Why are you isolating yourself from the rest of the crew?"

"I don't want anything to do with this crew." She shook his hand off. "Please leave."

He pulled a packet with two tranquilizers out of his pocket. "Here is something to help you sleep tonight."

She turned around and swatted the pills out of his hand. The packet ricocheted off the ceiling and stopped under the table.

"Go," she said, pointing at the door.

Randy left. He would have to come back and try again later. For now, he did not have good news to put in his report to Mission Control. His earlier reports about her unstable mental condition had kept the Air Force from making the crew search her room and imprison her, but they would have to if she did not improve soon.

⋐⋌⋋⋌⋌⋋

In the wardroom with the rest of the crew, Morgan strapped into the chair that Diego had bolted farther from the end of the table to make room for her pregnant belly. She picked at her lunch. While the world argued over the colonization of Mars, the Pax team was falling apart, thanks to her. Because she had decided to hunt for a flashing piece of metal, they had left Vlad behind, nearly left Diego, ruined Cass's career, and pushed Jamese over the edge.

She wished the Pax II team could at least have a peaceful trip home. First, they needed to get Jamese out of her room. Morgan didn't like Jamese, but the veteran astronaut was part of the team.

When Randy floated in, Morgan asked, "Is she coming?"

"No," he said. "She has totally withdrawn from us."

"Like a spoiled child," Cass said.

"*Si*," Diego agreed. "She needs a time out."

Randy shook his head. "We all need time alone, but not such a long time."

"Here's another message from Mission Control," Aiden said, holding up his notebook. "If Jamese doesn't come out today, they want us to search her room for artifacts and then guard her around the clock to make sure she doesn't take any from the storage containers."

"We can't do that," Morgan said. "We need to get her to rejoin us."

"How?" Randy asked. "I have been trying to convince her to eat with us every day."

Morgan unstrapped herself and floated up near Randy. "We should all try together."

"You're right," Cass said, also rising from the table.

"Jamese might have a serious psychological problem brought on by the stress of this mission," Randy warned.

"No, *amigo*," Diego said. "I think she's just mad at us. I'll go with Morgan and Cassi to make up."

"All right," Michelle agreed.

"I'm in," Aiden said.

Randy motioned that he would follow them, so Morgan led the way. She pulled herself along the handrails down the corridor to Jamese's room and then knocked on the door.

No answer.

"Maybe we should sing to her," Aiden said. "Is her birthday soon?"

"Come out, Jamese," Cass shouted.

"Lunch is ready," Michelle said.

"*Señorita*," Diego chimed in, "We are waiting here for your answer."

Morgan put her mouth near the door. "Please come with us to the table. I cooked lunch for you."

The door opened slowly. Jamese looked surprised to see all of them gathered outside. "Why do you want me to be part of the team after what happened?"

"Let's start over," Cass said with a big, warm smile. The rest of them smiled at Jamese, too.

She frowned. "Oh, all right. I'll eat lunch with you if you'll leave me alone the rest of the afternoon."

"Agreed," Morgan said.

CHAPTER 22

Vlad stood in front of Rockhouse and watched the sky through his helmet. A tiny star moved quickly among the familiar constellations. His visor display projected the trajectory of the supply ship, on its final orbit before landing. When the light disappeared around the other side of the planet, he wished the ship a safe descent and went inside.

℘℘℘

Two hours later, he was eating a packaged dinner at the wardroom table when the message from RKA arrived. *Greetings, Cosmonaut Kolovna. The landing of Kliper Ten at Cydonia was successful. You may proceed with our colonization plans.*

Greetings, comrades, he typed in reply. *I leave in the morning to start the first Martian colony for Mother Russia.*

He finished eating and headed for his room to sleep as long as he could before shutting down Rockhouse again.

℘℘℘

The next morning the small sun rose over the bright horizon while Vlad drove toward Sparrow. Full of as many extra tanks and supplies as it could hold, the lander stood ready to carry him to his new home. He parked near it and boarded.

After a smooth takeoff, he watched the craters inside Gusev shrink to pockmarks on his screen as Sparrow climbed into orbit. Vlad checked the coordinates of the Kliper Ten landing site, near the landforms that looked like pyramids. Maybe he would get to solve that mystery. He picked up the signal from the ship on the ground and then switched the controls to automatic. The computer would have to control his landing because he wasn't a pilot.

The ship's computer brought him down with the lander's big parachute deployed and retro-rockets firing. He prevented deployment of the air bags because they could cause him to bounce too far away. Sitting strapped into the only open seat among the extra tanks and supplies, he secured his helmet, braced his feet, grabbed the armrests, and waited for a rough touchdown.

"Landing complete."

The computer voice woke him up from a blackout. Even in the low gravity, Vlad knew his seat lay sideways. His extra payload must have unbalanced the ship, for another bad landing. The Americans should come up with a better lander design. One of the containers had broken its restraining rope. It must have knocked him out.

A long, vertical crack split his faceplate, which meant he was on cabin air again. He needed to get another helmet from the storage cabinet, behind his supplies. The cabin was probably still sealed, but he wasn't sure. Vlad unstrapped himself and quickly shifted containers and tanks until he could stand on the side of the lander. His head hurt. He checked the cabin's oxygen gauge to make sure he was getting enough air, but it was broken.

"American technology," he said. "Too delicate."

Trying to move faster, he shifted the cabin load until he could get to the spacesuit locker. "I should have left a path." He knew, though, that he couldn't have because every tank and container was necessary to keep him alive while he set up the habitat and power plant. At least he could keep busy until the other colonists arrived.

He exchanged helmets, did his safety checks with the computer, and cycled the air lock to go outside. The ladder stuck out into the air, so he had to slide over the hull to get to the surface. As soon as he stepped onto the ground, Vlad sent a voice transmission. "Greetings, all people of Earth. I claim Cydonia, the first human colony on Mars, for Russia."

He set up the portable habitat and then took a lunch break inside it. When he was full, he strapped on an extra oxygen tank and water bottle. Then he started the kilometer-long trek westward to his supply ship. He checked the coordinates of the ship against the map on his arm screen as he walked across smooth, red-brown sand that had a sprinkling of tiny gray rocks and shallow craters. A sky the color of fine single malt stretched above him. The "D & M Pyramid" should be a kilometer west of the ship, the "city square" a couple kilometers northwest of the pyramid landform, and the famous "face" a few kilometers north of the ship.

He would be the first person to explore these structures. Many people thought they were built by an ancient Martian race. Morgan should be here with him. At last he reached the silver ship, which reflected sunlight off its aerodynamic hull, and went through the air lock of the habitat module. It was going to be a long three months alone in the Cydonia colony until

his fellow colonists arrived. Vlad was grateful that he had a lot
of interesting work to do.

☙❦❧

Morgan was walking on the treadmill in the exercise
room, suspended in a harness, when her lower back started
aching. She slowed her steps. Maybe she should stop, but she
was supposed to walk 15 minutes longer. The pain moved
from her back around to her abdomen. She undid the harness
and floated away, holding her rigid abdomen with both hands.

Was this a contraction? No, it couldn't be. Not two
months early. They wouldn't reach Earth for another month.
Maybe it was false labor brought on by the exercise. She
would have to go rest to make sure she didn't have any more.

Sweat covered her clothes. She took clean shorts, socks,
and an oversized T-shirt from the supply cabinet, changed into
them, and put the dirty ones into the wall hamper. When she
started to leave the room, a wave of pain moved from her back
to her abdomen again. She curled into a fetal position, looked
at her watch, and concentrated on breathing. When the pain
stopped, she checked her watch again. Sixty seconds. She
pressed the talk button on the wall radio.

"Randy, I need help, fast."

A minute later he burst through the doorway, shoving
himself from the frame to her side. "What's wrong?"

"I had two contractions." Her abdomen tightened again.
She put his hand on it and bent over. "Here's another one."
The baby moved.

"Breathe with me," Randy said.

She did. When the pain subsided, she straightened her
body.

"You need to go rest." Randy steered her gently through the doorway. While they drifted along the corridor, he used his notebook to call the other crewmembers. "Morgan is having some early labor. I might need help in the medical bay."

Everyone met them there, even Jamese, who looked concerned. Cass and Diego looked scared. The next contraction hit Morgan after they strapped her to the exam table. Cass pressed a cool, wet cloth to Morgan's forehead while Randy checked her heart and then listened for the baby's heartbeat. The others hovered around them, closing in on Morgan. She wished they would wait outside.

"Breathe," Cass commanded. "Remember not to hold your breath."

The contraction stopped as soon as Morgan started her deep breathing.

"Here, take these," Randy said, handing her some pills.

"I'd rather not," she said.

"We have to keep you from having more contractions. Caring for a premature baby here would be risky."

"Drink this," Cass said, handing her a bag of water. "The rest of you, thanks, but please wait outside." The others left.

"Medication is the most effective way to stop premature labor," Randy said. "Also, I need to do a pelvic exam to determine whether the contractions have affected your cervix yet."

"All right," Morgan said. "But I want Cass to stay." Another contraction hit her, not as painful this time.

The exam was confusing and uncomfortable, like the regular exams he had performed, with her feet in stirrups and a light on Randy's forehead. All of this was necessary for the baby's survival, so she breathed deeply while Randy used an instrument to open her so he could reach inside. She did not

want to be intimate with him in this way. Cass squeezed her
hand in reassurance.

"Will you be done soon?" Morgan asked.

"Yes. I just finished." He withdrew his hand, stripped off
his rubber gloves, and covered her with a sheet. Cass stroked
her forehead.

"Am I in labor already?"

"I did not detect any progression of labor. We can try bed
rest and fluids first. If you continue to have contractions for
more than a few hours, you need to take the medication."

"That's risky for the baby."

"Being born prematurely millions of miles from the nearest hospital would be riskier."

"Okay. I'd like to try resting first."

"Good. We can start with some intravenous fluid here and
then move you to your room."

"I'll go tell everyone to stand down," Cass said as she
left.

Randy put a needle in Morgan's hand and set up an IV.
They waited silently while the fluid dripped into her. The contractions continued. Frequently he squeezed her hand or
touched her shoulder or cheek. She wanted to smile at him but
couldn't get the corners of her mouth to turn up. Before the IV
bag emptied, the contractions stopped, two hours after they
had started.

"Good job," Randy said. "I can take you to your own bed
now."

She held back her tears of relief while he took her back to
her room, until he left her alone there, tucked into her sleeping
net. Then she let herself cry and watched the drops of moisture
float around until she fell asleep.

෴

The emergency bells woke her up.

"Hull breach," the ship's computer said. "Please put on your spacesuits and helmets. Hull breach."

"Morgan, stay where you are," Randy's voice came over the radio.

She pressed the talk button and said, "I need my suit."

"Someone will bring it," he said. "Do not get up."

"What happened?"

Michelle's voice cut in. "He can't talk right now. A particle must have gotten through our ion shields. We don't know how much damage yet."

"Where is it?"

"The wardroom."

"Is anyone in there?"

"Jamese was cooking dinner. We haven't heard from her. I'll bring your suit as soon as I get mine on."

"I'm fine. My room is sealed. Go check on Jamese first."

"Randy and Cass went to get her."

Morgan lay back and waited, wishing she could help and trying to block out a fear that the ship would lose all of its air. She started hyperventilating, which wouldn't help anyone. Concentrating on breathing in through her mouth and out through her nose, she unfastened her sleeping net and started removing her clothes. She was in her underwear when Michelle barged through the door in full spacesuit and helmet, holding out Morgan's thermal undergarment.

"Hurry. The air is thinning. Get this on." Michelle helped Morgan dress and continued, "Diego is repairing the breach."

"What about Jamese?"

"She coded. They're trying to bring her back."

Morgan secured her helmet and moved toward the doorway. "We have to go help."

Michelle blocked her exit. "You need to rest and let them take care of Jamese."

"I'm fine."

"Randy doesn't have time for another patient right now. Please get back into bed."

"All right, but I want to help."

"We all do. You can help most by resting."

Diego's voice came over the radio. "The breach is sealed."

"Great work," Cass replied.

"How's Jamese?" Aiden asked.

"We have a heartbeat," Randy said. "But she hasn't regained consciousness."

Michelle helped Morgan fasten the sleep net over the spacesuit. "You need to keep your helmet on until we check the entire hull."

"I know. If I could have done my own chores, Jamese wouldn't be unconscious."

"What do you mean?"

"It was my turn to cook dinner, but she did it because I had early contractions."

Michelle smiled behind her transparent faceplate. "Thank goodness."

"I don't understand."

"Jamese might be okay now. Randy said if you had been in the wardroom when that rock cracked the hull, the baby would have died from oxygen deprivation."

"Oh." Morgan shivered all over. By nearly being born too early, the baby had saved himself. She hoped they could all make it to Earth safely now. "Thanks for helping me."

Michelle waved and left.

Realizing that Randy had been worried about her, Morgan set her radio to communicate only with the medical bay and pushed Talk again. "Randy?"

"Yes. How are you?"

"Good. Has Jamese opened her eyes yet?"

"Not yet."

"How long was she without oxygen?"

"About two minutes."

"Is that long enough to cause brain damage?"

"Probably not."

"Why did her heart stop?"

"The lack of oxygen caused a mild heart attack." He paused then added, "I will come by to check on you as soon as I can leave Jamese."

"I'm fine here. Thanks." She reset her radio to ship-wide communications.

Diego's voice came through the speaker. "Keep your suits on, everybody. We have some more holes to patch. Must have flown through a flock of meteors."

"How long until you can plug the holes?" Cass asked.

"Two or three hours."

"Okay. Everyone stay on suit air until then."

Morgan sighed. She tried to get comfortable against her bed, under the sleep net. Her stomach rumbled. The baby kicked. She sipped water from the suit bottle and then started to fall asleep. A contraction jolted her awake.

CHAPTER 23

Koll sat waiting in the middle of the conference table for what he hoped was his last meeting with NASA and Air Force staff. He wanted to be en route to Mars before Morgan returned and raised questions about why her blood samples got mixed up before the launch of Pax. If anyone suspected he did it on purpose to hide her pregnancy, he would lose his position as colony director and never make it to Mars.

The colony ship was scheduled to launch tomorrow, and the other seven colonists were ready to go. After that, a new colony ship would launch every two months. NASA staff had turned their exploration missions into transports for colonists and planned to maintain the same launch schedule as they had set for the explorations. Timon was still Mars Program Director, in charge of launches and space flights, so Koll needed to convince him that tomorrow's launch was safe enough in spite of the meteor stream that had hit Pax II.

Timon came in, sat across from Koll, and nodded. A good sign. Timon's managers filled the chairs beyond the two men to the end of the table opposite the big screen. Colonel Gray and his entourage, larger than usual today because of the impending launch, filled the other half of the table. NASA technical experts, administrative assistants with electronic pads, and other staffers sat or stood around the room.

Colonel Gray started the meeting the instant the door closed. No one was ever late to his meetings. "Director Brown, are we go for launch of the first Mars colony ship tomorrow?"

Timon glanced at Koll. Then he turned to Colonel Gray. "I think we need to discuss the problem Pax II just had before we decide the launch status of Pax III."

"Has Mission Specialist Kim recovered?"

"Yes, sir. She's back on duty already."

"Director Eriksen, what's the medical status of Mission Specialist Zeller?"

"The medication successfully stopped her premature labor. Dr. Arnold ordered partial bed rest until the birth, with no active duty."

"So the ship and crew survived a meteor shower that penetrated its ion fields, and they will probably make it back here before the baby is born." Colonel Gray folded his hands into one large fist on the table and asked Timon, "Were any of the artifacts damaged?"

"No, sir. None of the rocks hit the storage areas. We nearly lost Jamese Kim, though." Timon looked at Koll and then back at Colonel Gray. "Maybe we should do more analysis of the paths of meteor streams before we launch another ship."

Koll had been expecting Timon's suggestion. The director's caution had always kept the Mars program on a slow track. He didn't understand that sometimes people needed to take risks to accomplish great tasks. "In half a century, Pax II is the first ship traveling to or from Mars that encountered such a problem with meteors."

Kevin Wong, an expert on the trajectories of space objects, sitting in the corner between the windows and the screen, cleared his throat. "We don't know what happened to the Mars probes that disappeared."

Koll wished the young man would stay out of the discussion.

Colonel Gray swiveled his chair nearly backwards to face Kevin. "Mr. Wong, do you think meteors might have hit those spacecraft?"

"Yes. That's one of the official possibilities for loss of communications with each of the probes."

"Other possibilities include computer problems and component failures," Koll said.

"Another such meteor stream is unlikely," Timon agreed, looking straight at Koll. "But it is a risk."

Although Koll admired Timon's integrity, he wished his colleague had some concept of supporting him regardless of the issues. He had to convince Timon, who was supposed to be on his side now, as well as Colonel Gray. Twice the work. "The colonists and I are willing to take that risk, which is one among many risk factors."

"Can we reduce the risk of hitting a meteor shower by delaying the launch?"

"Maybe," Timon said.

Koll would have to appeal to Colonel Gray's patriotism. He shuffled his papers to find the latest report from Russia. "The Russian supply ship just landed, giving their colonist a base from which to explore and claim more territory." He handed copies of the report to the NASA manager on his right and the Air Force captain on his left to pass around. Electronic copies filled the tabletop. "Rather than delay our launch, shouldn't we set our flight schedule to catch up to the Russians? Couldn't the ground crew study the meteor paths after we launch? Then we could make a course correction, if necessary, on the way."

"Yes, that would be just as effective," Kevin said, surprising Koll.

The same kind of integrity that made Timon so cautious prevented Kevin from sticking to an argument when someone presented a more logical counter argument.

"I think it would be safer to wait," Timon said. "In midflight, our desire to continue the mission might affect our judgment. We need more data to make the right decision here."

"If you had more time, could you reduce the risk from meteor streams to zero?" Colonel Gray asked, rising to his feet.

Timon looked down at his hands. "We can never reach zero risk."

Koll held his breath, waiting for official approval.

Timon looked up at him. "I guess you have a go for launch, Director Eriksen."

"See you at oh-six-hundred for liftoff," Colonel Gray said as he marched out.

The NASA staff remained in their seats while the colonel's team filed out. Timon leaned back on his armrests and said to Koll, "I hope you understand the risks."

"Yes, I understand them. Every manned flight that we have sent to Mars faced greater risks. We improve the safety with each flight."

"True. Let's go back to my office for a bon voyage toast."

ᥱᢀᥱᢀ

On Mars, Vlad suited up in the exercise room and started going through his checklist. The wall screen beeped to announce a message from RKA: *Stay in your habitat until the colony ship arrives. Excursions without backup personnel are not authorized.*

They expected him to sit inside near the most intriguing sites on Mars and do nothing for more than ten weeks. The launch of the colony ship was already late because of hardware glitches. He removed his spacesuit and went to the wardroom in his thermal undergarment to see how much vodka he had. His comrades should have slipped at least a few bags of it into the storage compartment for him.

He found five bags, ripped open two, and drank them fast. He should probably eat some lunch, or at least put some clothes on. RKA might want a video of the lonely astronaut enduring hardships to do his duty for Mother Russia. Instead, he sang a drinking song.

On the wardroom table next to him, his pad beeped to announce the arrival of a new RKA message:

> *The Americans just launched a colony ship, a week before we can launch ours. Proceed with your explorations. All excursions are authorized. Keep us informed of your progress.*

Vlad went back to the exercise room and suited up again. He fastened his helmet and started out the air lock door. As he stepped onto the first ladder rung and saw the clear, salmon-colored sky, a hissing noise tickled his ear. His heart skipped. He hadn't performed the safety checks. Vlad punched the door button, but the air lock didn't slide open. He used both arms to push his helmet farther around and fasten it securely.

The hissing stopped, but Vlad lost his balance and fell two meters to the surface. He landed with his left leg twisted under him. Pain shot from his ankle up through his calf and knee, ripping a scream that no one else could hear from his throat. His sight dimmed. When the agony subsided, he tried to see if his suit had torn but couldn't focus on the task. His head throbbed with his leg. The searing pain in his leg engulfed him again until he wanted to escape into blackness. He struggled to remain conscious until he knew the suit was intact. Even the smallest tear could mean death if he didn't fix it.

A pinprick of cold just below his left knee scared him into alertness. He pressed his left glove hard against the spot, starting another wave of torment and dizziness. Nausea brought bile to his mouth. With his right glove, he fumbled for sealant fabric on his utility belt, tore off a strip, moved his left hand, and taped the cold spot.

Sobering fast, Vlad realized why the air lock wouldn't open. He had pushed the button before the air recycled. This was a stupid thing for a man alone on Mars to do. At least he hadn't turned on his radio yet, so RKA hadn't heard him yell.

He straightened his legs, yelling at the pain in his left calf. He tried to stand by pushing up on his hands. Even in the lower gravity of Mars, his left leg wouldn't bear any weight. It must be broken. His gut twisted.

He waited for the anguish to subside enough to calm his stomach so its contents wouldn't emerge into his air supply. When the pain was barely tolerable, he pulled himself very slowly over the magenta sand and back up the ladder, glad that his arms were strong from two hours of daily exercise. This time the air lock opened, and he was safe again.

How could he report this progress to RKA? "I was drunk and forgot the procedure" wouldn't sound right. He had to think of something, after he found some Vicodin and splinted his leg.

ᘒᘒᘒ

An hour later Vlad reported his broken leg, leaving the vodka and hissing helmet out of the report. He slipped, that was all. Everybody slips sometimes.

The return message read, *Rest until you can proceed with explorations on a rover.* That meant they expected him up and hopping around within a few days. He would have to design a walking splint that would fit inside his spacesuit.

ღჳღჳ

Resting upright in her room near the wall screen, Morgan plowed through page after page of messages, answering some and saving or deleting others. After reading the announcement of the successful launch of the first colony ship, she sent a message to Koll to congratulate him. Her message would travel millions of kilometers from the mail server on the inbound Pax II to the mail server on the outbound Pax III, without going through the Earth systems.

The message from Vlad on the fourth page punched her in the gut.

> *I need you here to help me explore the strange land forms. When I tried to do it by myself, I "slipped" and broke my leg.*

She knew that the quotation marks around "slipped" meant that he had been drinking and lost his balance. She replied that she missed him and hoped he could stay inside his habitat until his leg healed.

If she hadn't insisted on looking for that piece of metal, which he helped her find, Vlad wouldn't be stranded on Mars. She wished she could turn the ship around and go back after him. Morgan was afraid she would never see Vlad again.

She set her wall radio to communicate with Randy in the medical bay and pushed the talk button. "Do you have a few minutes to come by?"

"Yes. I am on my way."

He arrived before she finished reading her messages. "Are you having more contractions?"

"No. The medicine worked. Did you get a message from Vlad?"

"Not today, but I heard that he broke his leg."

"I feel terrible that we left him."

Randy put his arms around her. "He chose to stay."

It felt good to be held, but Morgan moved back a little because she didn't know exactly what kind of relationship she had with Randy. Also, she wanted to see his face while they talked.

"Are you planning to go back?"

"Maybe. Are you?"

"Yes, I want to go as soon as the baby is old enough to travel. My family will go to help me with him. I don't want to be part of this fighting over which country sponsors which colony, though. I wish all of us could have stayed at Rockhouse together."

"Even Jamese?"

"Jamese helped us keep organized. Our team was stronger because it combined the strengths of every person in it."

"And the weaknesses. I think you are forgetting some of the problems we had."

"No, I'm not. Part of our strength was how we helped each other cope with our weaknesses. Now we're not there to help Vlad when he needs us."

Randy reached out his right arm to grasp her shoulder. "Vlad is a strong man, a survivor. He will be there when we return."

She put her hand on top of Randy's. "So you've decided to go back to Rockhouse?"

"Tentatively. I thought you would rather settle in Cydonia, though."

"The Russian colony." Did Randy mean he wanted to go to Rockhouse while she went to Cydonia, or did he want to settle down with her and the baby?

"I think Vlad would make room for us," Randy said. "Maybe if we ignore colony sponsorship, the people of Earth would start to ignore it, too."

Randy had said "us." Morgan nodded, smiled, and moved closer to him. She still had to tell him he was the baby's father, though, and he always got angry when she withheld information from him. This information could end his career with NASA, so maybe she should continue to let everyone think her fertility procedure succeeded.

A new message from Koll's assistant, Marcia Reynolds, flashed across her wall screen. It confirmed what she had suspected. Koll had withheld information about her pregnancy to further his colonization plan, just as she had kept the baby's paternity a secret to protect Randy's career.

୧୬୧୬

Two weeks later Vlad put on the new skinny splint, suited up, and went through all his safety checks. Then he hobbled into the air lock with a crutch under his left arm. He waited for the air to cycle out, opened the hatch, and tossed the crutch out. Using his arms and good leg, he safely descended the ladder to the rusty ground. Finally, he could start unpacking the supplies and stock the rover. With only one useful leg, it took him three hours to get the rover out of the equipment module of the ship, test the motor, and pack it with supplies, extra tanks, and a portable habitat. When he finished, the ache in his injured leg made it difficult to limp back around to the ladder on his crutch. He needed more Vicodin.

ഇഇ

That night the RKA message mapped out an exploration plan for him to follow the next few days. They wanted him to proceed to the "face" and then the "city square," but he wanted to go to the pyramid first. All his life, he had followed orders, but why? His latest reward was to be left alone on Mars, with no help when he needed it. Now his government insisted that he start exploring before his leg healed, which could cause more injury or even death.

If he continued being a loyal Russian citizen, he would be participating in the fight over who owned which colony. Mars would end up just like Earth, with people attacking each other to claim pieces of ground. Why couldn't they all own it together, like when he lived in Rockhouse with the Americans and the French lady? Were they not all people?

His government was using him, like the United States was using its people, to set up another war zone. He wanted no part of it. Not tomorrow, not ever again. Tomorrow he would go explore the pyramid landform, because he wanted to. When his friends returned to Rockhouse, he would join them there and then bring them to see the wonders of Cydonia.

Vlad shut down his computer. He would not send any more messages to Earth, either. Let them all think he was dead. Then they couldn't use him to fight with each other. He went to the viewport to look at the most beautiful star in the sky, Mother Earth.

CHAPTER 24

Randy was climbing into his sleep net when someone knocked on his door. He climbed back out, stretched lengthwise toward the door, and opened it. "Hi, Jamese."

She dangled in midair before him in her tight pants, red shirt, and bare feet. "I need to talk to someone."

"The wardroom would be a good place to talk." What did she want now? Just a week away from Earth, he had hoped they would not have any more problems. What could she want to talk about with him alone?

"Somebody might be there getting a snack," she said.

"We can use the medical bay, then."

"Oh, all right." She floated down the hall ahead of him, her hips undulating as if she were swimming a butterfly stroke. Smiling back over her shoulder, she batted her eyelashes at him.

He pushed the handrails to catch up and float above her. "Are you sure you just want to talk? If something else is on your mind, you are wasting your sleep time. Nothing has changed."

She turned onto her back underneath him, bringing her face only a few inches away from his. "Yes, I just want to talk. Isn't that part of your job, to listen to us?"

"Yes, if you are sure that is all you want to do."

"Are you accusing me of improper behavior? If you don't want to talk to me, I can call Mission Control and ask for a psychiatrist to talk to. The time delay won't make much difference this close to home."

"No. Sorry. I just thought—"

"Because I look pretty, you assumed I wanted to sleep with you?"

They passed the turn that led to the wardroom. He looked left and right. No one seemed to be within hearing range, but in these close quarters, he needed to be sure. "I can answer that as soon as we have more privacy."

At the end of the corridor, they floated up to the medical bay. He opened the door and motioned for her to precede him. After he closed the door, she locked it and started taking her clothes off. Her spicy scent filled the room.

"Stop undressing."

"Why? You said you wanted privacy, so I assumed you wanted to make love."

"You know I did not mean that." Her behavior was becoming irrational again. He had to choose his words carefully.

She took off her underwear and lay naked against the paper sheet stretched over his exam table.

He grabbed her bra and panties as they floated by his head and tried not to look at her body, which swayed from one side of the table to the other. "Please put these back on."

She rose up a few inches as if levitating and bent double to strap her ankles into the table stirrups. Her petite breasts touched her knees. Then, like a gymnast on a balance beam, she reached over her head and did a backbend to grasp the side handles near the end of the table.

The underwear glided out of his hand and behind him.

"I don't think I can tolerate any more rejection." Her ivory face shone with lust. "Please, could we just have a few moments of pleasure together? It would help us release our built-up tension. No one would ever find out, and we would both feel better—kind of like an internal massage."

"I would know," he said. Careful not to float near her, he gathered her drifting underwear from behind him and pushed it her way. "Please put your clothes back on so we can talk."

Morgan's voice came over the radio, "Randy, are you in the medical bay?"

Jamese grinned.

Randy flipped the talk switch on the wall. "Yes."

"I forgot to pick up my medicine. I'll come get it now."

"You need to rest, Morgan," he said, making eye contact with Jamese. "I can bring it later."

Jamese unstrapped her ankles and crossed her legs into a lotus position in midair, still naked, resting a hand on each of her knees.

"OK," Morgan said. "If you're coming by soon. I'm sleepy."

"Good night," Jamese said, her dark eyes twinkling.

"Who's that?" asked Morgan.

"I have a private consultation," he said. "I can bring your medication soon." He turned off the radio.

How was he going to get away from Jamese without making her state of mind worse? He wanted to know what Morgan was thinking. She must have recognized Jamese's voice. He needed to get this consultation under control.

"We can talk about your tension, but that is all," he told Jamese. Backing up against the wall, he knocked loose a bedpan, which floated into the other wall and ricocheted to the door, where he caught it. He strapped it back on the wall.

"You don't have to throw things at me," she said in a matter-of-fact tone. "If you don't want me, just say so." She retrieved her clothes and started dressing. "You're no fun."

He managed to suppress his relief. "This is not about fun. I told you that I care about Morgan."

"Then why don't you tell her? If you really have made up your mind between us, why doesn't she know?" Jamese pulled her pants and shirt back on, took a standing position against the table, and reached behind herself to hold onto it, making her breasts stand out under her shirt.

"Because I care about you as a friend and did not want to upset you."

"Upset me?" Her voice rose as she spoke. "Do you think I'm so easily upset—a scientist and experienced astronaut? Do you dare to assume that how you feel could upset me?"

"What is causing you so much tension?"

Her pale face colored and her voice got louder until Randy was sure that everyone on the ship could hear it. "You are. You need to make up your mind, now."

He spoke in a low voice to try to calm her. "This discussion is supposed to be about your problems and concerns. What can I help you with?"

"You and Morgan are my problems. If you really wanted her, you wouldn't leave her alone all the time. You can help me with my tension. I know you want my body—you watch it all the time. What's the big deal about spending a few intimate moments together?"

"It would not be right—"

A knock interrupted them. He was glad for an excuse to end the conversation, which was not improving Jamese's mood.

"We could hear Jamese from the wardroom," Cassandra said through the door. "Are you guys all right?"

Jamese removed her shirt again and ripped it. "Help me. I said no, but he wouldn't stop."

"What?" Randy stared at her in surprised disgust. He flung open the door.

Behind Cassandra in the corridor, Diego's eyes grew larger and larger.

"Jamese has become irrational," Randy said. "I think we need to confine her to her room for the remainder of the flight."

"You try to rape me and you call me irrational?" Jamese's voice sounded calm and indignant now. "I think we should confine you to protect the women." She pulled her shirt back on, with extra cleavage showing through the tear, and pushed past them out of the room. "I'm going to report this to Mission Control."

"What's going on?" Morgan asked from the end of the corridor.

"You need to keep your man under control," Jamese said as she passed her.

"Randy? Cass? What is it?"

"We can take care of this," Cassandra said. "Go back to bed."

"No. Tell me what happened, Randy."

"It would violate doctor-patient privilege to discuss my session with Jamese."

"Your session?"

"Yes, Jamese came to my room for a consultation. I suggested we go to the medical bay."

"Why would you do that?" Morgan asked, concern tightening her face.

"It is a more appropriate place for a session." Randy felt guilty for causing Morgan anxiety when she needed to be calm. He hoped the guilt was not apparent to the others because they might think it had something do with Jamese.

"*Amiga*," Diego said as he sailed by Cassandra and took Morgan by the arm. "I can help you get to your room so you can rest."

"I've been resting. I want to know what happened here."

"I cannot tell you," Randy said.

"If you don't explain," Cassandra told him. "We have only Jamese's story to go by."

"I can tell you that it is just a story."

"I thought so, but she's going to make sure it goes on your record. She might even press charges."

"What story?" Morgan asked.

Cassandra sighed and took Morgan's hands in hers. "Jamese accused Randy of attempted rape."

Randy's stomach lurched. He wondered what Morgan was thinking. Her face looked blank. She turned away from him without a word and moved slowly toward the sleeping quarters, keeping her left hand over her distended abdomen. He wished he could hold her and soothe her pain.

∞∞∞

Morgan knocked on Jamese's door, determined to straighten out the accusations against Randy. Her back hurt, and she felt exhausted, but this couldn't wait.

"Go away," Jamese said.

"Open the door," Morgan said.

"I don't want to talk to you."

Morgan turned and pulled herself along the handrails to her room as fast as she could. Poising herself in front of her wall computer, she shut down the mail server. She changed the security on the server files so that no one except her could start it up again. Then she relaxed in the air and waited for Jamese.

Five minutes later someone knocked. She opened the door to a scowling face.

Jamese zoomed in and pointed at the computer. "You blocked my message to Earth and locked me out of the mail server. Start it up."

"You don't want to send that message."

"Why not? Randy attacked me, and I need to report it."

"Nobody on this ship believes you."

"Mission Control will believe me."

Morgan held her right palm out to Jamese. "We're supposed to be a team."

"What would you know about teamwork? You've controlled this entire mission and grabbed all the glory of our discoveries for yourself. You even managed to cheat me out of being the first colonist. I was supposed to step on Mars before anyone else."

"I don't care about who is first. Can't we just—"

"Then you won't care if I jettison your precious artifacts." Jamese sped through the open doorway, into the hall.

ళుళుళు

Strapped to his desk chair on the colony ship, Koll hoped he and the other colonists would be able to get to Mars on schedule, before the Russians took over. In ten weeks he would realize his dream of landing on the red planet. He went over the plans for the first few months. He wanted the colony to get all life support systems fully functional before the next group of colonists arrived. The Air Force would want his team to search for more alien artifacts, too.

His wall radio came on. "Koll, this is Timon."

Koll reached up to press the two-way, encrypted communications button. "Yes, I'm here."

"We've detected a meteor stream that could pierce your ion shields."

"Have you told our pilot?"

"No. There is only a five percent chance that a rock would get through the shields."

"You won't alert him unless the odds are ten percent, right?"

"That's the mission profile. I don't think we should take even a five percent risk, though, when we don't have to."

Koll frowned. Timon's excessive caution always made the job more difficult. This time Koll might have to order a change in course. "How much would a course correction delay us?"

"A month. Colonel Gray said it's your call. The Russian colony ship would reach Mars first if we made the correction, so he's not in favor of it. I've sent you the data."

Koll opened Timon's message on his screen and clicked the attachment. The new trajectory would take them into a less-traveled area of interplanetary space. "I'm looking at the data now. How can we be sure we won't run into a more dangerous meteor stream along the new course?"

"We can't. Kevin's group is still trying to project the paths of all known objects in that area."

"And there might be unknown objects?"

"Yes, maybe. But we are certain about a potential danger along your current trajectory."

"We always have potential dangers out here." Koll closed the meteor simulation and Timon's message. "If the Russians arrive before us, they could claim Gusev Colony as well as Cydonia. I think five percent is an acceptable risk."

"I had hoped you wouldn't decide that," Timon said. "But my team and I are here to help you however we can. We'll keep running projections of the meteor paths."

"Thank you."

℮⁄ᴐ℮⁄ᴐ

Morgan pressed the general alarm button next to the radio over her bed. Then she set the communications to ship-wide and pressed the talk button. "Everyone to the cargo hold, fast."

Her room was closest to the hold, so she reached it before the rest of the crew, in spite of her bulk. Jamese wasn't there. Soon the others arrived.

"What's wrong now?" Cass asked.

"Jamese threatened to jettison the artifacts."

"She must be suiting up," Aiden said.

"Diego and Michelle, stay here and keep her out of the cargo hold," Cass ordered. "Randy and Aiden, come with me to the exercise room. Morgan, go back to your quarters and rest."

If Morgan argued with Cass, it would keep her from finding Jamese when every second was critical. She nodded and turned toward her room. On the way back, she slipped through an open hatchway right when Jamese, already in her spacesuit, floated by with a container. "She's here," Morgan broadcast through her wrist radio as she turned around.

Jamese floated away down the corridor, pushing the container in front of her.

"She's headed toward the backup air lock."

Morgan followed Jamese through the corridors to the air lock on the other side of the ship. Jamese closed the door in Morgan's face. From the locker next to the air lock, Morgan grabbed the largest suit. She started suiting up, never taking her eyes off of the transparent chamber door. Jamese hooked a cable to her belt and then threw a switch. Air began emptying from the chamber. Morgan secured her helmet and set its radio to full communications.

"Jamese, please stop," Morgan said as she pulled on her gloves. "We can talk about this."

Ignoring her, Jamese grabbed the floating container and punched the button to open the outside door.

"Cass, please help me with my safety checks."

"I'm almost there."

"No time." Morgan went through the safety checks over the suit comm while Jamese floated through the outer doorway with the container, into space.

Jamese's backpack came loose and started to drift away. She hadn't gone through the safety checks with anyone. If she lost her air, she'd have to rebreathe her suit air until she returned to the air lock. Jamese let go of the container and grabbed for her backpack, sending herself into a spin that yanked her belt off, leaving her gyrating around the container. The cable end snapped the empty belt back into the air lock.

Morgan wondered if the alien ring was in that container. How could Jamese pull such a stunt when they were almost home? She always found a new way to cause trouble. Finally, Morgan realized she was not the one at fault for most of their difficulties. Jamese was. Shaking herself into action, Morgan pressed the button to close the outside door and re-pressurize the chamber.

"Jamese, you need to breathe slowly to conserve the air in your suit," Morgan said, following emergency training to keep a person at risk focused on procedures. Why should she endanger her child to save someone who kept her from Randy and made her life so miserable? She'd rather let Jamese spin away from the ship permanently. But Morgan knew she couldn't do that, even though the aftermath of Jamese's tantrum put all of them at risk. The woman needed psychiatric treatment, partly because she had lost everything she wanted to Morgan. "We're coming to bring you inside."

Cass arrived with Randy and Aiden.

"You cannot go out there," Randy told Morgan as he reached for a suit.

"I have to. She might not last until you're ready."

Cass nodded. "We're right behind you." She and Aiden started suiting up, too, in the corridor.

Morgan entered the air lock and grasped Jamese's belt from midair. She undid the cable end, felt below her huge belly for her own utility belt, and secured the cable to it while the inner door closed.

The distance between Jamese and the container must have increased. Morgan would be able to reach only one of them. If she brought the container back, she would probably get a commendation from NASA, but that would be risking a human life for a thing. She pointed her body toward Jamese's last position and punched the emergency exit button to open the outer door without emptying the chamber air. The out-gushing air propelled her near Jamese. After winding the cable around the other woman and stopping her spin, Morgan pulled both of them back in hand over hand along the cable length.

As soon as they returned to the air lock, the outer door closed. Air filled the chamber again. She waited for the pressure light on the wall to turn green, then removed Jamese's helmet. Randy rushed in. Jamese was unconscious but breathing.

"Are you all right?" he asked Morgan. She nodded.

"Aiden, help me get Jamese to the medical bay," Randy said. They carried her away.

Even unconscious, Jamese could come between Morgan and Randy. Ashamed of herself for the selfish thought, Morgan let Cass remove her helmet and help her out of her suit.

ↃↄↃↄↃↄ

The alarm bells jolted Koll out of a pleasant daze as he was waking up. His adrenaline brought him to full alertness and made his heart beat fast while he pulled on some sweatpants. As mission commander, he was responsible for the crew's safety.

"Hull breach," the computer said. "Hull breach in the exercise room."

No one would be able to get to the suits in there, unless they were already exercising. Restraining an urge to panic, Koll punched the ship-wide communications button on the wall radio. "All crewmembers, this is Commander Eriksen. Go to the secondary air lock and put on your backup suits. Let the automatic system seal off the breach."

"Okay," the pilot said.

"Roger," the copilot chimed in.

Koll zoomed out of his tiny compartment and along the corridors to the exercise room, strapping on his wrist radio as he went. Trying to remember the crew's exercise schedule, he hoped no one had been in that room. Fear pulsed inside him. He sent another ship-wide broadcast. "Remember your training. Check in with me now. As soon as you have your suits on, go through the safety checks on your way to the medical bay. You'll be safer there, in the middle of the ship."

After the crewmembers responded over the radio, Koll's fear came to life. Sandi hadn't checked in. This was probably her exercise time. He pulled against the side rails to increase his speed, thinking five percent wasn't really an acceptable risk when the worst happened. Who was he to take such risks with other people's lives? First, he had manipulated Morgan into a pregnancy away from the normal support systems on Earth. Now he had gambled that they would be safe from meteor streams and lost.

When he reached the corridor outside the exercise room, the airtight window revealed Sandi pressed sideways into half-closed inner air-lock doors in a spacesuit, her eyes rolling in terror. He saw the hull breach, above and behind her helmet, a black spot on the outer doors. Red lights blinked in the air-lock chamber in time with the alarm bells, flashing the color of blood over her white suit.

The gauge on the wall showed the oxygen content and air pressure dropping in the room. The hole in the outer door must have created enough suction to pierce the inner seal just as Sandi finished putting on her suit. Her body must be blocking most of the tear on the inner seal, but not all of it. The force of the suction would eventually pull the rest of the seal through and then Sandi, piece by piece. Her wild eyes told him she had figured this out. She reached toward him.

"Sandi, try to stay calm. I'll get you out of there."

"No," she said. "It would be suicide. I'll try to pull myself along the side rails toward the door."

"The automatic system won't let you open this door. I'll have to seal the corridor doors first and override the system from here."

"Then what? You don't have a suit."

"I'm working on it. Please try to stay calm."

Koll hurried to the doors and used the wall panels to seal each of them. Shivering without a shirt, he checked the air in the exercise room. Less oxygen than on top Mount Everest. From a supply cabinet in the wall, he grabbed a respirator mask and the end of a roll of rope. Then he punched the code in the wall panel to override the automatic seal. Nothing he could do about the air pressure. Sandi waved at him to get back, her flailing arms and legs making her look like bait on a fisherman's hook.

He had to fix this. It was his responsibility. He'd taken too many chances with other people's lives.

The doors whooshed open. The rush of the denser air from the corridor almost pushed him into Sandi. Fighting to move his fingers fast in the cold air, he tied the rope to her belt, tested the knot, and pulled himself back along the rope to the corridor, behind the wall. He jerked hard on the rope with his left hand to yank her through the doors and then punched the button with his right to close them. She banged against the walls, back and forth across the corridor, as the air stabilized, but he was too tired to stop her. He just hoped she was all right.

"Commander Eriksen, what is your status?" the pilot's voice came over the radio. "Sandi?"

"I'm okay," she said.

Okay. Sandi was safe now. Soon they would all be safe on Mars. Koll hoped Morgan would never find out what he did to her. She had always been a good friend.

"Commander Eriksen?" It was Sandi's voice again. Strange how her voice came over his radio when she was right next to him. Why didn't she take her helmet off? Was the light still red? The alarm bells had finally stopped.

Koll closed his eyes. His body felt good floating in the warmer air, but his head ached. He just needed some sleep. Overwhelmed by exhaustion, he drifted into unconsciousness.

એન્ડ

On Pax II, Morgan asked Randy over her room radio about Jamese's condition, hoping she was better. Morgan was concerned, but she also wanted to know if Randy would be able to take a break and come by soon.

"No change," he said. "She is still in a coma, but we are moving her to her room now. Maybe the specialists on Earth can help after we land."

"Thanks for the update."

"Please try to rest. I can inform you if anything important occurs."

"All right."

He wasn't coming. She tried not to think of the long, lonely hours ahead of her. They would be back on Earth in seven days. Her baby would be born a month later. His tiny foot pressed under her left upper rib bones as he squirmed inside her. It must be his foot because Randy had told her the baby's head was down now, already positioned for his birth.

Close to tears because of her increased hormone levels, she forced herself to go through her breathing exercises. She didn't want to do this alone anymore. She was sure Randy cared, but he had been more concerned about everyone else's reactions than her feelings. Maybe he didn't care about her as much as he'd claimed. Ashamed of these thoughts, she tried to reason with herself. Randy was right to be concerned about Jamese's mental state. It was his job, and her own actions had pushed Jamese over the edge, endangering her life, but he was trying to help her.

Morgan's laptop beeped to announce the arrival of a message. On her screen, a new message from Timon was marked urgent. She opened and read it.

Mission Control regrets to inform you of the
loss of Dr. Koll Eriksen due to an accident on

Pax III. A small meteor penetrated the outer door of the air lock next to the exercise room. Dr. Eriksen gave his life to save Mission Specialist Sandi Kapoor, who had been exercising when the meteor struck. She was able to don her spacesuit before the air started leaking through the inner door seal, but the suction trapped her against the seal. Dr. Eriksen, without a spacesuit, coura- geously brought her back to safety but was over- come by cold and low air pressure. Pax III is con- tinuing to Mars, in his honor, where the crew will lay him to rest at Gusev Colony.

Morgan started crying. With tears floating around her, she pressed the talk button to speak with Randy again. "When you get Jamese settled, would you please come by my room?" She sniffed. "I need you."

"I can be there in a few minutes," he replied.

While she waited, she cleaned the tears from the air with a hand vacuum, thinking about Koll and their long friendship. He had been her base doctor since she started working for NASA. She would never get to join him on Mars to help build his vision, the new colony, which he had described in detail to her. Now the gathering on Mars when she went back would be incomplete. Koll would never see her son.

Soon Randy arrived and took her in his arms. She pointed to the message on her screen. As he read silently, she put her head on his shoulder and cried some more, letting his shirt soak up her tears.

"I need you, too," he said. "We are both going to miss Koll, like we miss Vlad."

She looked up. "Vlad might still be all right."

"Yes, he might. We have to worry about you now."

"About me?"

"Yes. You are about to give birth to your first child."

"My first? Does that mean you want—"

Randy stopped her words with a kiss. "Would you like to go to the wardroom for a while? Everyone will gather there."

She nodded. "Who's taking care of Jamese?"

"We stabilized her and left the radio on in her room. I have mine on to hear if she wakes up." He showed Morgan his wrist. "Also, she is connected to monitors, so I can check her vitals on my pad. She will probably be unconscious until we land."

They went to the wardroom, where the rest of the Pax II crew sat around the table. Morgan and Randy joined them in a toast to Dr. Koll Eriksen.

Sitting next to Randy in silence while the others chatted, she wondered what he had meant when he said she was having her first baby. It would be his first one, too, but he didn't know that yet. He hadn't let her finish her question. If she told him that he was the baby's father, would he want to be a part of her life, to raise their child together? She would have to tell him soon.

CHAPTER 25

Finally orbiting Earth, Morgan and the rest of the Pax II crew prepared for reentry. She sat strapped into her cabin seat in her spacesuit, with her helmet on her knees. The baby's foot lodged under the top of her rib cage, on the left, so she leaned on her right arm. Her belly stretched halfway to the seat in front of her, where Aiden sat. Randy typed rapidly on his keyboard in the seat to her left. Her uterus contracted.

Morgan checked her watch and fought the urge to hold her breath. Sixteen hundred hours. The contraction lasted forty-five seconds. Maybe it was an isolated one. They were almost home. If the baby could just wait a few more hours.

The rest of the crew flipped switches, typed on keyboards, moved levers, and talked to Mission Control.

Six minutes later she had another contraction, a full minute long, and then another, stronger one five minutes after that. She grabbed both sides of her abdomen, leaned back, and moaned.

"Are you all right?" Randy asked.

"Nooooo." She breathed in through her nose and out through her mouth until the contraction stopped.

"How many? How far apart."

"I've had three contractions six and five minutes apart. Ow. Here's another one."

He undid his seat straps and held her shoulders. "Breathe."

"I know—ouch."

"Someone tell the ground," he said. "I am not sure we can stop the labor this time."

"Mission Control," Cass said over the radio. "We have a woman in labor here. Do you copy?"

Even without a communications delay, the reply came several seconds later. "Yes, Pax II, we copy you. A discussion is under way. Ask Dr. Arnold if he has anything to delay the birth until after you land."

Cass looked up from the console. Randy held Morgan's hand while she breathed in short gasps.

"It is probably too late," he said, shaking his head. "I recommend continued orbit so I can perform an exam to find out."

"Mission Control, that's a probable negative," Cass said. "Dr. Arnold requests permission to continue orbiting so he can do an exam to confirm."

"We need to land now," Morgan said. "I can't have this baby in space. How am I going to push it out?"

"With your muscles," Randy replied. "That is why you did all those exercises."

"Pax II, this is Mission Control. Permission to orbit granted for as long as you need to. The pediatricians are talking about whether the baby should come down later or go to the space station until he can adjust to gravity. Keep us advised about any change, and good luck."

Morgan gripped Randy's arm as another contraction started. She had lost control of her labor and delivery. After the contraction subsided, Randy and Cass helped her move to the medical bay.

❧❧❧

As soon as they strapped her to the exam table, pressure rose up her abdomen and around to her back.

"Look into my eyes," Randy said as he stretched out and floated beside the table. He began to breathe in and out with her.

Morgan focused on his eyes, two pools of green light that kept her safe through the waves of pain. She matched her breathing to his until the contraction went away.

Wetness gushed between her legs, and the moisture started spreading up her gown. Droplets of moisture floated away in every direction.

"What's going on?" Aiden asked from the doorway.

"Her water just broke," Randy replied. "Everyone put your helmets on and grab the vacuums. Cass, please tell Mission Control we are not landing until after the baby is born."

"They know. We're streaming all communications to there for doctors."

"No," Morgan said. "Why?" No one had asked her. This was supposed to be a private time. She could endure giving birth on a spaceship because it was too dangerous for the baby to go through a landing after her water broke. But she couldn't stand every sound she made being recorded for posterity.

"Colonel Gray's orders," Cass said. "In case something goes wrong."

Morgan didn't like it, but she would not object again. They were already being recorded, and she wasn't going to let anything spoil the birth of her child.

Members of the crew floated in a circle around Morgan, hooking their feet wherever they could to leave their hands free. A vacuum in each hand, Diego grinned as he joined the hunt for droplets.

"That one's getting away," Michelle said.

"Got it," Aiden replied.

"Here comes another contraction." Morgan breathed with Randy, her eyes locked onto his, while the crew flailed about cleaning the air.

"All clear," Cass said as the contraction subsided.

"Not for long," Randy sighed. "This was just practice. Would someone please find something to put the baby in? And Morgan, will you marry me?"

The surrounding astronauts looked at each other. Michelle reached for an object wrapped in plastic in the corner.

"Here." She gave it to Randy. "This is my mother's prayer shawl. It was sterilized for the trip, so I thought you might need it."

"Thanks." Randy turned to Morgan, who was staring out the viewport. "Well?"

"No. I can't marry you while I'm having a baby," she said, embarrassed that the NASA and Air Force staff members were listening to every word. "Oh, oh. This one is worse. Help me."

"Breathe," he said, taking her hand again.

The crew moved out into the corridor.

When the contraction subsided, he performed a pelvic exam. Then he wiped the sweat from her face with a washcloth. "Marry me because I love you,"

"You really love me?" She wished they weren't having this conversation in public. "Why?"

"Why?" He gripped the side of the table. "How can I answer that? I don't know why. I just love you."

"How can you love someone who is such a mess?"

"You will really be a mess soon, but this is only temporary. You have already dilated to four centimeters. Can we please get married before transition?"

"Where's Cass? I don't want it to be like this. I love you, too, but we should have a wedding after we land."

"We can have an elegant wedding ceremony later, but I want to get married here first, for the baby. The first citizen of space should have a father."

"Let's not talk about the father." She couldn't let him throw away his career. If it was all right not to know who the father was from a fertility procedure, it should be all right not to tell anyone that that Randy was the father. She would tell him later, when he retired from the space program.

"I know I am the—"

"Randy, don't."

"I am the baby's father." He smiled at her. "I do not care who is listening. I want the whole world to know. Please do me the honor of becoming my wife."

"Maybe in a few minutes. I need to get ready first."

"You are beautiful just as you are "

She punched his stomach. "No, I mean I need to get ready for this contraction."

He gasped and doubled over without breaking eye contact with her. "Look at me and breathe. Start panting."

"Pax II, this is Mission Control requesting a status report."

In her spacesuit, Cass floated toward the console while the contraction subsided. "Vacuums," Randy shouted. Then he turned to Cass and said, "Can you marry us now?"

Cass winked as Randy ducked a floating particle. "Mission Control, this is Pax II," she said. "We're planning a wedding here, followed by a birth."

Droplets of blood floated past Morgan's head. Space-suited figures with vacuums filled every corner of the room.

She started panting again, resisting the urge to push. Randy stayed with her, holding her hand.

"Pax II, this is Mission Control. Please give our best to the bride and groom. We are preparing a family honeymoon suite on the space station for their arrival. After the baby is born, you can dock with the station. We'll find a way to bring the rest of you down to Earth."

"We copy," Cass said. She moved to Morgan's left side and began the wedding ceremony. Michelle gave Morgan a silk flower. She and Randy repeated their vows between contractions.

Cass pronounced them husband and wife, Randy kissed the bride. Then he did a pelvic check.

"Push," he said.

An orbit and many vacuum bags later, baby Rand Arnold Zeller became the first person born in space. He looked perfect, swaddled in Michelle's lace shawl as Morgan nursed him. He was extra-long for a newborn though. Randy measured him at twenty-three inches.

☙❦❧

President Cole called the newlywed parents to extend her congratulations. Morgan and Randy thanked her.

"Have you considered returning to Mars as the first colonists?" the president asked.

"We're still discussing our options," Morgan said while rocking her sleeping baby in her arms.

"Yes, Madam President, we need a little time to plan our future together," Randy said.

"Please decide quickly. The Chinese colony ship might beat Dr. Eriksen's ship. Also, Russia just launched their colonists, who will attempt to claim Rockhouse for their country because Vladimir Kolovna never left Mars. He might be alive.

"How does that affect us?" Morgan asked. She could not give away Vlad's secret plan to start an independent colony on Mars, even to the President.

"You and Rand are the first colonists, without dispute," Cole replied. "The United States clearly owns Rockhouse as well as all the territory bounded by the places your team explored. If you go back right away, we can extend that before more countries establish claims.

"Have all the countries agreed not to take their conflicts to Mars?" Morgan asked.

"We're still trying to get a number of them, including China and Russia, to sign the treaty."

"So the only ones who signed are countries without their own space programs," Randy said.

"Well, our Congress is still debating the terms," the president said. "Please let me know as soon as you make a decision."

"We will," Morgan and Randy said together.

"America honors your service and regards you and your crewmates as heroes. Goodbye."

"Thanks," Morgan said.

"I am honored to serve," Randy said. "Goodbye."

Rand stirred in Morgan's arms, under her sleep net, and started to cry.

Randy reached out, and Morgan put the baby in his arms. He checked the diaper, cut from a spacesuit undergarment, and grinned. "Looks like little Rand did not like what the president said, either."

"So you don't want to go back?" Morgan asked.

"That depends on what you want. How do you feel about being used to gain more territory?" Randy started changing Rand, which stopped his crying.

"I won't let them use me. I want to raise a family with you, but I can't settle on Earth while a war I started rages on Mars." Her eyes filled with tears. "If we go back, though, it might be too dangerous for Rand."

The baby sucked his fist while Randy cleaned him.

"Wherever we go, it might be dangerous, especially because we are in the middle of this. We might be a target for terrorists."

"I know," Morgan said. A few tears drifted up as she recalled the sight of her grandparents' car plunging through the Golden Gate Bridge to their ocean grave amid clouds of smoke. Her heart had become a chasm of grief that day.

"I have an idea," she said. "Maybe we could return to Mars without being part of the U.S. colony. Vlad said he has room for us."

"You want us to be part of a Russian colony?" Randy asked.

"No. Vlad doesn't want any part of a government territory, either. He wants to live there on his own and has invited us to join him in Cydonia."

"How can we do that?" Randy asked. "When the Russians find out he is alive, they will say he stole their equipment and supplies and that the colony is still theirs. They could even claim Rockhouse and the surrounding territory because he stayed on Mars."

"We can use the alien artifacts to get all of the countries to agree not to nationalize any colonies."

"But we have to turn over the artifacts as soon as we reach the space station." Randy cradled sleepy Rand in his arms.

"Let's not," Morgan said. "If our crewmates agree, let's use our discovery to bargain for peace on Mars."

"That would really put us in danger, with no protection from anyone. They were willing to sacrifice Diego and Vlad to get the artifacts back."

"Yes, we would be in more danger if it doesn't work."

"Also, why would all the countries agree? Only the U.S. would have the artifacts."

"We can ask that all countries be given access and that we, our families, and our friends get passage to Mars as well as everything we need to set up our own colony with Vlad."

"They will never agree to all of that."

"The governments won't, but the people will. They know that the wars are wrong, and they think of us as heroes."

"We are not heroes."

"No, we are explorers who have a chance to give humanity a better start on Mars because of what we discovered there. We have unique leverage, artifacts that everyone on Earth wants to examine. The governments want to know if the aliens might be a threat to us, and the people want to get to know our space neighbors."

"All right," Randy said. "I will go ask the rest of the crew if they are in." He swaddled Rand in an adult T-shirt and settled him next to Morgan. "You take a nap."

As Randy sailed out the door, Morgan tucked the dozing baby back into the sleep net with her, holding him face out. She laid her head back against the air pillow, wondering how she could secure the artifacts if the other astronauts did not agree with her plan.

CHAPTER 26

On the way to the space station, Morgan wondered how the governments would react to the ultimatum she was about to give them. She finished nursing Rand in the communications seat and then handed him to Randy. Although her abdomen and pelvis still ached from childbirth, she released her seat buckle and straightened to a standing position to deliver her message.

Her crewmates had already agreed with her plan and set up the ship's computers for a full video broadcast to Earth, the moon, and the space station, with an Internet feed, as Jamese had done for her broadcasts from Mars. Even Vlad could listen from Cydonia, to a delayed signal. Now she turned on the equipment to send a message that would either save Mars from colonial war or land the Pax crew in the brig.

On her left, Cass smiled up from the command seat, next to Diego, who nodded from the pilot's seat. Randy stood on Morgan's right, his Velcro boots pulling up from the floor rhythmically as he rocked the baby. Behind her, Michelle sat beside Aiden, who was eating something crunchy that smelled like cheese. Everyone looked ready for her to begin.

"Governments of Earth, this is Morgan Zeller on Pax II. As you know, the crew and I returned from Mars with alien artifacts. We also returned with a vision of a peaceful Mars, not owned by any Earth country, in keeping with the Outer Space Treaty of 1967. Many of you have ratified this treaty.

"We've all seen what happened to the lunar settlements. In spite of the Moon Agreement of 1979, the settled territory is divided by country, and conflicts that started on Earth continue between the lunar colonies. During my two months of training there, the U.S. base came under attack three times, and we returned fire. Since then, explosions in outposts on the moon have killed a dozen people from five different nations."

While she spoke, Timon rushed into the Mission Control room in Houston, where everyone stood behind their consoles, staring at the large screen.

"The Pax crew and I were planning to return the artifacts to the U.S. government, the sponsor of our international mission. These artifacts, though, belong to all the people of Earth, as do the moon and Mars, according to our own treaties."

At Mission Control, Timon asked, "What's she doing, Flight?"

"She's making an unscheduled speech," the flight director for the mission, Gustav Krantz, said.

"Tell her to stop and check with us first."

"Yes, sir. CapCom, ask her to hold up until we discuss this."

"Okay." Melinda Stevens, the communicator, said over her comm unit. "Pax, this is CapCom. Do you copy?"

As Timon waited for Cassandra's reply, he listened to Morgan.

"As I speak," Morgan was saying on the screen, "colony ships from several countries are on their way to Mars to claim territory and set up military defenses. The United States is attempting to claim a colony in my name, even though our mission had crewmembers and equipment contributed by different countries. If we don't want Mars to become as dangerous as Earth, we need to stop the land rush."

From her station at Mission Control, Melinda said, "They're not responding, sir."

"Keep trying, and somebody interrupt that broadcast."

"What's going on?" Colonel Gray yelled from the doorway as he swept into the room, flanked by two aides, all in uniform.

"We're trying to find out, sir," Timon said.

"The Pax II crew wants the artifacts that we found to be shared by all countries," Morgan said, her face smiling above them, "in exchange for their agreement to abide by the settlement treaties. We want the lunar bases returned to their original scientific purposes and any colonies on Mars to be strictly for exploration and settlement, not to become extensions of Earth countries.

"We also ask for a safe return to Mars to establish our own colony there, for ourselves and any family members and friends who want to go with us."

"Have they all gone crazy up there?" Colonel Gray asked. "Stop this right now."

"We're attempting to interrupt the broadcast. How's that going, Flight?"

"It was set up so that no one can stop it," Gustav replied.

"Find a way," Colonel Gray ordered Timon. "Or I'll have your jobs for this."

"I know," Timon said. Out of options, he watched Morgan reach out with both hands.

"If you want to help, you can ask your government to agree and sign the treaties. No matter what happens, it is vital that we all remain peaceful. Mahatma Ghandi and many others have shown us how. Please avoid violence.

"We have an opportunity here and now to stand up for a peaceful colonization of space, an opportunity that might never happen again. This might be dangerous, but the survival of your descendents could depend on it.

"Everyone, please let us know what you decide by the time we reach the space station. We have set up our website for you to vote yes or no, and we will support your decision. We ask all governments to support what their people decide. Zeller out."

On Pax, Morgan strapped herself back into her chair, trembling and exhausted. Her crewmates clapped. Now everything depended on the reactions of the people on Earth.

e∕ɔe∕ɔ

Five hours later Pax II docked with ISS. Suited up, with her helmet and gloves attached to her belt, Morgan held one end of an enclosed, pressurized bed where Rand slept. She went through the air lock, while Randy maneuvered the other end of their child's space cradle. At the sight of the station astronauts and cosmonauts, joy filled her. They had come home. She and Randy set down the cradle in the space station, and she hugged him.

The station crew had no welcoming smiles, though, as they helped the Pax crew out of their spacesuits. Randy undid the seals on Rand's bed and handed the baby, still asleep, to Morgan. She held him close.

"Did you hear Morgan's message?" Cass asked Colonel Alex Sidharov, the station commander.

"Everyone heard it," he replied, still unsmiling. "Unfortunately, we have a message for you from NASA."

"Why wouldn't NASA send the message directly to us?"

"Sadly, Commander Cassandra Nickels, my orders are to relieve you and your crew from duty and place you under arrest. I'm to take command of Pax II as well."

"My ship? No, you are not going to command my ship or arrest my crew."

"I'm sorry," Colonel Sidharov said. "Those are my orders."

Morgan handed her sleeping baby to his father, nodded at the cradle and then the hatch, and moved to the viewport. She watched their fragile planet turn, hoping Randy would put Rand back in the pressurized bed and leave.

"Colonel," she said. "Have you seen the explosions on Earth lately?"

"Yes. Another war is breaking out in the Middle East."

"The people causing those explosions are following orders."

"Of course. They are soldiers."

Morgan searched her mind for what to say next. How could she convince this dutiful cosmonaut to help them?

"When people follow orders, other people tend to die," she said. "The wars are getting worse. How long do you think civilization will last if people keep following orders?"

He joined her at the viewport and looked out. "I'm sorry, Mission Specialist Zeller."

"Should we keep following orders until we destroy our world and the moon?" she continued. "Will we take the wars to Mars and destroy it, too?"

The colonel motioned to the U.S. astronauts assigned to the space station to take the Pax crew into custody.

"We're not going to fight you," Cass said. "But we are going back to our ship."

Randy was already pulling the cradle through the air lock. Cass caught the other end to help him, with Diego close behind.

Morgan tried to follow, but the colonel blocked her way. The station crew surrounded Aiden and Michelle.

"We can create a peaceful future on Mars, Colonel Sidharov," Morgan said. "I think the people of Earth are with us even if the governments are not. We might never get another chance."

"You said that already in your message," he told her. "Please come with me. We have secure quarters ready for you, with fresh clothing."

"Cass, close the air lock and keep our guys safe," Morgan said over her radio. "The rest of us are going to extend our visit on ISS."

As they moved through the air to the crew quarters, avoiding the equipment that covered every surface, Morgan tried once more to convince the colonel. "Please check our website and the newscasts to see the response of the people. Will you do that for me?"

"I will," he said. "You are so brave, and your discovery has already changed the world."

"So far, it has started a fight over Martian territory."

They stopped beside a locked hatch in the crew quarters. He unlocked the hatch and motioned for her to go in.

"For you, our space mother," he said, smiling, "I will check your website and the news."

e/೨e/೨

She floated into the tiny room. Sidharov closed the hatch, and a lock clanked into place. When had they added locks to the station rooms? Her breasts, swollen with milk, started to ache. Separated from her baby, she held back hot tears that stung her eyes. Randy would find a way to feed Rand, but her arms were empty. She longed to be with them now. Why was she trying to save Mars when she had a baby to care for and a new husband?

She knew why. Her discovery had started the land grab. It was her responsibility to try to stop it.

She removed her spacesuit, hung the pieces on hooks in the corner, and peeled off her insulated undergarment. Then she checked the clothing cabinet and found a dark blue shirt, shorts, and socks in her sizes. While pulling them on, she looked around.

This room must have computer access. Every room on the station did. She started trying the wall panels. One of them slid open at her touch to reveal a screen, but no controls.

"Turn on," she said.

The screen lit up. She would have to use voice commands.

"Website Pax Flight."

A Google logo flashed across the screen before it filled with the home page of the site they had set up for the mission. She had expected some response to her speech, but the numbers were unbelievable. About twenty million positive responses so far, and only a million negative.

"Television CNN."

The news report stunned her. It showed people flocking toward their government capitals all over the world, as her speech replayed in a small window at the top right of the screen. The confirmation that so many people agreed hardened her resolve to see the plan through, even if she remained locked up.

She had never intended to lead a revolution, but this had to be done to save them all from self-destruction. Koll Eriksen would be proud of her. His colony ship would reach Mars soon. She wished she could be back at Gusev Crater when they laid his remains to rest there.

"Scan news stations."

The computer showed one station after another. The coverage was all about people leaving their homes in pilgrimages to their centers of government. In Washington, D.C., many thousands already surrounded the White House and the Capitol.

In Beijing, tanks rolled toward crowds of citizens.

Big Russian guns fortified Moscow against a massive gathering.

A throng in New Delhi chanted, "Peace on Mars," in English and, according to the news report, in Hindi, Urdu, and Punjabi. The report added that the chant was spreading to other countries, with demonstrators around the world repeating, "Peace on Mars," in their own languages.

Tears floated freely from Morgan's eyes as chills ran up her spine. The people had taken up her cause. Maybe the governments would listen. She hoped no one would get hurt in the demonstrations but knew that some probably would.

She had to get the station crew behind the plan. How? All astronauts and cosmonauts wanted peaceful extraterrestrial settlements, but they also had to follow orders to remain on the active crew lists. Maybe if she showed them what was happening in their own countries and states, they would agree with the ultimatum. She could also invite them to join the Cydonia colony. Vlad would not object to having more trained workers there.

First, she had to get out of the locked room. The uncomfortable pressure in her breasts reminded her that it was Rand's feeding time. She set her radio to broadcast just to the station and Pax.

"Colonel Sidharov," she said. "This is Morgan. I need to nurse the baby."

His reply came swiftly. "Then someone will have to bring the baby onto the station."

She left the radio on as she gave a computer command.

"Prepare broadcast to all receivers on Earth and the moon. Security lock Randall."

"What are you doing?" the colonel's voice demanded over the radio.

"I'm going to let everyone know that I'm separated from my baby and cannot nurse him. Milk leaked from her breasts onto her shirt. She took a picture of herself and sent it to all the station and Pax screens

"We are stopping all broadcasts," Sidharov said.

"My security lock will prevent that. After I feed Rand, I want to have a discussion with you and the rest of the space station crew. Please let me out so I can transfer to Pax."

"If I do, you will not return."

"Yes, I will. I want a chance to convince all of you to help us."

"How do we know you will return?"

"I'll leave my spacesuit."

The door opened. Sidharov hovered in the opening.

"We cannot help you, Morgan, but we will listen when you return."

He had never used her first name before. Maybe the sight of guns over Red Square on the newscasts had affected him. He moved aside and motioned for her to go.

"Thank you, Alex," she said.

℮ↄ℮ↄ

In Randy's room on Pax Two, Morgan waited while he changed Rand and then handed him to her. She kissed Randy. He folded down the chairs from the wall, sat in one, and smiled at them.

Rand cried. She took the other chair and nursed him. His tiny fingers uncurled in relaxation as the pressure in her breast decreased. Would this be the last time she could hold him? Her heart full of love for her son, she wanted to enjoy every second of his tiny, warm body in her arms. She wished she could escape back to Earth with him and Randy and live there together, but she had to protect Rand's future. If something happened to her, Randy would take care of their boy. She had to continue with the plan.

Rand fell asleep. Grateful that he had a healthy appetite, she returned him to his cradle.

"What happened on ISS?" Randy asked.

"Let's close the cover to keep out the noise," she said. "I need to get back soon. Should we take him to the crew cabin so I can tell all of you at once?"

Randy nodded, closed the clear cover on the cradle, and turned on its air cycling system. Morgan watched the tiny sleeping face while they carried the bed along the corridor.

Cass and Diego sat in front of newscasts on the main screen. People walked toward their government capitals and rode by bicycle, car, and bus. "All flights are booked, all trains are full, and still people are finding ways to travel," a reporter said. The screen showed horseback riders and donkey carts full of men, women, and children. Morgan wondered if the demonstrations would be safe for the children.

Heavy security laced the crowd in Washington, D.C., with the Metro Police and U.S. Park Police deployed throughout the National Mall and Capitol. Guns pointed above people's heads everywhere.

"The FBI and Homeland Security have issued a security bulletin," Jamison Robles said. The reporter Morgan had met the day she joined the Pax mission, after the bomb had injured Sandi, stood facing a camera with the massive crowd as a backdrop. "The national guard has been called up here and in every state to protect the capitals."

The screen showed soldiers with guns arriving at Capitol Park in Sacramento, California, only ninety miles from her parents' home. She wondered if they had gone to the park.

"How are Aiden and Michelle?" Cass asked as Diego switched off the video.

"I didn't have any contact with them," Morgan said. "But I was treated well. No one even tried to block computer access."

"Because they know it wouldn't do any good," Diego said. "You would take apart the wall to find a terminal."

Morgan started laughing with them, but stopped quickly. The laughter sounded nervous, and they didn't have much time. She had to go back in a few minutes.

"You heard most of what went on," she said. "They can't block us now without shutting down their own computers. I'm going to try to convince them to join us."

"How can you do that?" Cass asked.

"I'll show them what's happening where they live, if they haven't already seen it. Maybe that will work."

"You're not going back." Randy put his long arms around her, as if they could keep her on Pax.

"Yes," she said, melting into his strong chest. "I gave my word, and left my spacesuit."

"We have a spare one here," Cass said.

"I can't stay here until we get Aiden and Michelle back."

"We can figure that out together," Cass said. "Morgan, you—"

"Don't order me not to go, Cass. I don't want to disobey your orders."

"Getting the crew back is my job."

"Then tell me what to do when I go back."

Diego looked down and shook his head.

ৎ৯ৎৎ

When she returned to ISS, Morgan asked for a meeting with all the station crew as well as Aiden and Michelle, as Cass had suggested. Colonel Sidharov agreed. They all gathered in the Tranquility module, where land and sea passed by in the view of Earth through the Cupola windows.

As the astronauts and cosmonauts arrived, Aiden and Michelle brought up three different news channels on the monitors just below the windows, with the sound off. Cass had thought of this, too.

"Thanks," Morgan said. "Please keep switching the channels to show the crewmembers their homelands, as much as you can."

"Okay," Michelle said, without smiling.

Aiden, still calm in the midst of this crisis, winked and gave Morgan a thumbs up.

Morgan lowered herself below the observation deck to address the crew, but before she could begin, Sidharov spoke.

"Mrs. Zeller-Arnold, we will listen to what you have to say out of respect, because you asked us to. We admire your achievements. But do not think you can influence us with your words." He looked at his socks. "We must follow our orders." Then he pulled his head up to look at her, his eyes speaking his anguish. "You and your crew are still under arrest."

Most of the men and women around her looked resigned or uncomfortable, but some looked angry. She didn't know if they were angry at her or for her.

Fear covered Michelle's face as she held the rail on the left of the screens with one hand, a remote in the other. Aiden, on the right, looked up at the view of Earth.

"You are a good soldier, Colonel Sidharov," Morgan said, discarding the prepared speech in her head. "All of us are here because we have a duty to our countries, but should we be serving the corrupt governments who would leave a cosmonaut in a dust storm to get what they want, or should we serve the people of our countries?"

She pointed to the newscasts above them. Aiden turned up the volume on CNN with the remote.

"Peace on Mars," the chant continued. Demonstrators had kept it going all over the world for hours. Michelle and Aiden kept switching stations on the monitors to show the astronauts and cosmonauts their national and state capitals.

"This is what the people want," Morgan said. "It's up to us now."

"What do you mean by 'leave a cosmonaut in a dust storm'?" Sidharov asked. "Your commander and pilot searched for Vladimir Kolovna until you had to leave."

"We were ordered to leave him and Diego there. Cassandra went down against orders to bring them back. She found Diego, but the storm was too intense to even attempt to search for Vlad before they had to leave. Mission Control said they would bring the ship back remotely if Cassandra and Diego didn't return in time."

"We were told every effort was made to find Vlad," Sidharov said, suspicion narrowing his eyes.

"That's my point," Morgan said. "Governments tell us what's in their own best interests, to perpetuate their power. We have to decide for ourselves what is right."

"I have always followed orders."

"Would you have followed the orders to fill Vlad and Diego's seats on the main lander with artifacts and leave them on Mars when the second lander couldn't fly through the storm?"

"I don't know." Sidharov shook his head and looked down. The crew around him murmured to each other.

"I always followed orders, too," Morgan said. "But I wish I hadn't that time. Vlad was like a big brother to me. It took me a while to realize that returning the artifacts was more important to the U.S. government than returning its people. If aliens are in our solar system now and the governments find out, what do you think they'll do?"

"Try to communicate with them?" Maria Riano, a U.S. astronaut, said.

"Is that why they sent guns and bombs with the colony ships?" Morgan asked.

"The weapons are to protect themselves against the colonists from hostile countries that are on their way to Mars," Sidharov said.

Morgan pointed at the newscasts, where millions of voices chanted, "Peace on Mars," as tanks and soldiers with guns continued to form lines between them and the government buildings. "Are they drawing weapons against hostile countries now?"

Guns erupted on one of the screens. People fell to the ground. Some of the watching crewmembers gasped.

"They are firing on their own people," Morgan said, her eyes filling with tears. "The death toll from the demonstrations is rising." A number flashed on the screen. "The longer we delay, the more the demonstrators are at risk. People don't want to live with terrorism or war anymore."

"Turn up the volume on the left," Sidharov commanded.

Michelle muted the middle monitor and brought up the sound on the left one, where tanks had started rolling in Red Square, directly at the crowds. People stood and started backing away from the tanks, but with millions behind them, they had nowhere to go.

"They can't do that," Boris Karanovich, a cosmonaut pilot, said.

"Someone must have given them an order," Morgan replied, keeping her voice soft to avoid angering the Russians.

The tanks continued their relentless, slow movement toward the crowd. People climbed over each other, pushing against the throng to get away. Morgan hoped they could find a way to save themselves, but she couldn't think of any that didn't involve fighting back, and the protestors were not armed. Maybe the tanks were just trying to scare them away.

"If they don't stop soon, hundreds of people could be crushed," a man with a Russian accent was reporting in English. A tank advanced on him. "We have to leave now." He moved sideways, but the camera still showed the impending massacre.

Just before the tanks reached the edge of the crowd, it started receding rapidly.

"What happened?" Sidharov asked.

"Crowd surfing," Aiden said, a slow smile spreading across his face.

A thrill of relief and hope filled Morgan. People had listened to her and found a way to resist without fighting. Michelle looked at her with red-rimmed eyes and nodded.

"What do you mean, 'crowd surfing'?" Boris asked.

Aiden gestured at the screen. "The people near the edge are lifting the people in front over their heads and passing them back to others, like people used to pass each other up to the stage at a concert."

The newscaster reappeared in a small box on the top right while hundreds of bodies moved back across a sea of hands. "This is an incredible sight in Moscow. It looks like people are swimming on top of each other. They seem to be moving back fast enough to avoid the tanks.

The ISS and Pax crews watched in silence until Red Square was clear of demonstrators. Throngs filled the streets of Moscow, but the tanks stopped at the edges of the square, in front of St. Basil's Cathedral, the State Historical Museum, and other buildings.

"I see what you mean," Sidharov told Morgan. "But you are asking us all to give up our careers. If we join you, we can never go back home to our families."

Morgan smiled and opened her arms. "Then come with us to Mars, and bring your families."

"You still don't know if NASA will let you take the ship. I will have to think about this," Sidharov said. The rest of the ISS crew seemed to agree with him. He floated to the doorway and nodded at Morgan, Aiden, and Michelle. "For now, you will remain under arrest. If you need anything, let us know. Maria and Boris, would you please escort our guests to their quarters?"

After the colonel pushed himself into the hall, Maria said, "I'd really like to go with you, Morgan, but if this global demonstration falls apart, they're not going to let any of us go. We need to wait until NASA and the governments decide." Other crewmembers nodded.

"I know I'm asking you to risk everything," Morgan said. "If you don't stand with us, we'll lose the only leverage we have to get the governments to agree with a peaceful settlement of Mars. The people are already demanding it all over the world, but that's not enough. We need the ISS crew with us so NASA can't take the artifacts by force. The return ship with armed guards will be here soon."

"I'm going to wait for the colonel's decision," Boris said.

ᏜᏜᏜ

On Pax to nurse Rand again, while Michelle and Aiden remained captive on the station, Morgan watched the news in the control room with Randy, Cass, and Diego, while Jamese slept in her room.

The death toll from the demonstrations was more than a thousand now and rising. The news stories showed that some deaths were accidents, but in some countries, troops were firing on the crowds. The shooting pushed people back but did not end the demonstrations. Morgan felt sick inside. What had she started? How many people had to die for peace while she sat here enjoying her new baby, safe at least until the return ship arrived?

"Mission Control to Pax II," the radio blurted.

Diego answered, "Pax here."

"The President wants to speak with Morgan."

"Roger that," Diego said.

He handed a communications cap to her.

She shifted Rand to one arm and put the cap on with her other hand.

"Hello, Madam President. Zeller here."

"Hello, Morgan. The United Nations has authorized me to deliver a message to you. They have drafted a new agreement for the peaceful settlement of all extraterrestrial bodies and sent it to every country for ratification as a treaty among nations."

Relief coursed through Morgan's body like a cool ocean breeze. "Please convey my thanks and appreciation to the United Nations delegates for their fine work."

"The United States Congress and I also have a message," President Cole said.

"Yes?"

"They unanimously approved your proposals for sharing the alien artifacts with all other countries and for providing a safe return for you to Mars, as well as transportation for any family members and friends who want to join you. The legislation provides for enough equipment and supplies to sustain your colony until it gets established. NASA, which is no longer under the Air Force, will make the arrangements. Also, all military bases will be dismantled on the moon. I just signed the bill."

"Thank you." Morgan held her baby close and looked at the smiling faces around her as everyone cheered. "The Pax crew thanks you, too."

"I would say you're welcome, but we didn't have much choice," the president replied. "You are all very brave. I want to thank every one of you, our finest Earthlings, as we send you out to become Martians. You have risked everything to set us on the right path for settling new worlds."

"We appreciate all your hard work to get the legislation passed," Morgan said, as tears of joy wet her cheeks, and Randy hugged her shoulders. Rand slumbered in her left arm with no awareness that his entire future was being decided on this day.

"Thank you," the president said. "Now, will you please send the rest of our citizens back to their homes? It's getting crowded around here."

Morgan, Randy, Cass, and Diego laughed.

"Yes, Madam President," Morgan replied. "I'll set up a broadcast right away."

"Thanks again. It has been a pleasure knowing you. Please stop by my house the next time you visit Earth. Goodbye, Morgan.

"Goodbye. Zeller out."

Everyone rushed to hug Morgan. Aiden, Michelle, and then the ISS crew poured in through the hatch, yelling, "Congratulations, Morgan," "You did it," and other words of praise.

Colonel Sidharov squeezed into the crowded crew cabin last. "So, we begin a new adventure," he said. "This time without guns."

"Yes," Morgan agreed. "But first we have to thank the people of Earth. Aiden, is the broadcast set up?"

He nodded.

With the astronauts and cosmonauts surrounding her, she began her message to the demonstrators all over the world.

"Fellow citizens of Earth, the Pax and ISS crews cannot thank you enough for your courage and sacrifice to keep our wars from reaching Mars. My president has just informed us that the military bases on the moon are closing, and I hope the fighting will soon end on our home planet.

"Those who died or sustained injuries during this difficult time have given themselves to help us learn to live together in peace. I regret the loss of so many people in the demonstrations and extend my deepest sympathy and gratitude to their loved ones. If you have been injured, please be well soon, and know that your suffering will make life better for us and for our descendants.

"Everyone who helped bring about the peaceful settlement of other worlds in any way should be very proud. You made a difference, maybe even stopped us from destroying our species. You have done enough for now. Please go home and celebrate this momentous achievement with your families and friends, and honor those we lost in the struggle.

"Some of us are going on to Mars, where our families and friends can join us. We hope to see many of you there."

THE END

About the Author

Bonnie Vaughan became fascinated with space travel when the first lunar lander took off from the moon, a feat she had thought was impossible. As the author of numerous newspaper and magazine articles, her most exciting interview was with Colonel Al Worden, pilot of the Apollo 15 command module, who told her how fragile the Earth looked from a distance.

A journalism degree from San Jose State University landed her a job as a technical writer. While writing her own science fiction stories on weekends, she authored many software books for Silicon Valley companies. She received an Award of Distinguished Technical Communication from the Society for Technical Communication and was honored as an Achiever by the Santa Clara branch of the National Association of American Pen Women.

Her hero is Dr. Harrison Schmitt, the geologist who walked on the moon.

www.bonniegvaughan.com